PATRICK'S DESTINY

Center Point
Large Print

Also by Sherryl Woods
and available from Center Point Large Print:

The Chesapeake Shores Series
The Inn at Eagle Point
Flowers on Main
Harbor Lights

The Devaneys
Ryan's Place
Sean's Reckoning
Michael's Discovery

**This Large Print Book carries the
Seal of Approval of N.A.V.H.**

PATRICK'S DESTINY

SHERRYL WOODS

CENTER POINT PUBLISHING
THORNDIKE, MAINE

The text of this Large Print edition is unabridged.
In other aspects, this book may vary
from the original edition.
Printed in the United States of America
on permanent paper.
Set in 16-point Times New Roman type.

ISBN: 978-1-60285-885-5

Library of Congress Cataloging-in-Publication Data

Woods, Sherryl.
    Patrick's destiny / Sherryl Woods. — Center Point large print ed.
        p. cm.
    ISBN 978-1-60285-885-5 (lib. bdg. : alk. paper)
    1. Family secrets—Fiction. 2. Large type books. I. Title.
    PS3573.O6418P38 2010
    813'.54—dc22

                                                              2010020963

PATRICK'S DESTINY

THE DEVANEYS

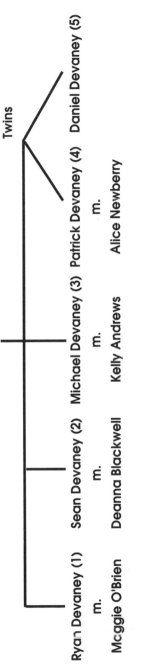

Connor Devaney m. Kathleen McDermott

Ryan Devaney (1)
m.
Maggie O'Brien

Sean Devaney (2)
m.
Deanna Blackwell

Michael Devaney (3)
m.
Kelly Andrews

Patrick Devaney (4)
m.
Alice Newberry

Daniel Devaney (5)

Twins

(1) Ryan's Place
(2) Sean's Reckoning
(3) Michael's Discovery
(4) Patrick's Destiny
(5) Daniel's Desire

Chapter One

Spring came late to Widow's Cove, Maine, which suited Alice Newberry just fine. Winter, with its dormant plants, icy winds off the Atlantic and stark, frozen landscape, had been more appropriate for her brooding sense of guilt. The setting had been just as cold and unforgiving as her heart.

But she was working on that. In fact, that was the whole reason she'd come home to the quaint Victorian fishing village where many of her female ancestors had lost husbands to the sea. Eight years ago she'd had a bitter disagreement with her parents and left, determined to prove to them that she could make it on her own without any help from them.

She'd done it, too. She'd worked her way through college, gotten her degree in early childhood education and spent several years now teaching kindergarten, happily nurturing other women's children. She'd assumed there would be ample time ahead to make peace with her parents, many more years in which to have a family of her own.

Then, less than a year ago, on a stormy summer night, John and Diana Newberry had died when their car had skidded off a slick road and crashed into the sea. The call from the police had shaken Alice as nothing else in her life ever had, not even that long-ago rift when she'd been little more than a girl. Not only were her parents dead, the chance for reconciliation had been lost forever. So many things between them had been left unspoken.

From that instant, a thousand *if onlys* had plagued her. It tormented her that they'd died with only the memory of her hateful words echoing in their minds . . . if they'd thought of her at all.

Alice had wondered about that. She'd been haunted by the possibility that they'd pushed all thoughts of her completely out of their heads on the day she'd climbed onto the bus leaving Widow's Cove for Boston. While she had lived with a million and one regrets and too much pride to ask for forgiveness, had they simply moved on, pretended that they'd never had a daughter? The possibility had made her heart ache.

When their will had been read, she'd had her answer. John and Diana Newberry had left everything to her—"their beloved daughter"—and that had only deepened the wound. For eighteen years she'd been their pride and joy, a dutiful daughter who never gave them a moment's trouble. And then she'd gone and they'd had no one left, at least no one important enough to bequeath their home and belongings to. She'd had to face the likelihood that they'd been not just alone, but lonely, in her absence.

Coming home after the school year to settle their affairs, Alice had spent a lot of time in the cozy little house on the cliff overlooking the rolling waves of the Atlantic and tried to make peace with her memories . . . of the good times and the bitter parting. She'd realized by July it was something that couldn't be accomplished in a few weeks or even a few months. So she'd applied for a teaching position in Widow's Cove and come home for good in August.

This first school year in Widow's Cove was passing in a blur, the seasons marked only by the falling of the leaves in autumn, winter's frozen landscape and her own unrelenting dark thoughts.

Now, finally, in mid-April, spring was creeping in. There were buds on the trees, lawns were turning green and daffodils were swaying in a balmy breeze. She hated the fact that the world was having its annual rebirth, while she was as lonely and as tormented by guilt as ever.

Worse, as if to emphasize how out-of-step she was with the prevailing spring fever, her kindergarten students were as restless as she'd ever seen them. She'd broken up two fights, read them a story, tried vainly to get them settled down before lunch, then given up in defeat. The noise level in the classroom was deafening, an amazing accomplishment for barely a dozen kids. Her head was pounding.

Desperate for relief, she clapped her hands, then shouted for attention. When that didn't work, she walked over to the usual ringleader—Ricky

Foster—and pointedly scowled until he finally turned to her with a suitably guilty expression.

"Sorry, Ms. Newberry," he said, eyes downcast as the other students promptly followed his lead and settled down.

That was the wonder of Ricky. He could stir up mischief in the blink of an eye and just as quickly dispel it. He could charm with a smile, apologize with utter sincerity or assume the innocent face of an angel. A child with that kind of talent for leadership and spin control at five was destined for great things, assuming some adult didn't strangle him in the meantime.

"Thank you, Ricky," she said. "Since it's such a lovely day outside, it occurred to me that perhaps we should take our lunches and go for a walk." Maybe the fresh air and exercise would work off some of this pre-spring-break restlessness and she could actually teach something this afternoon. Maybe it would cut through her own malaise as well.

"All right!" Ricky enthused, pumping his fist in the air.

A chorus of cheers echoed his enthusiasm, which only made Alice's head throb even more. Even so, she couldn't help smiling at the children's eagerness. This unchecked excitement and wonder at the world around them was exactly what had drawn her to teaching kindergarten in the first place.

"Okay, then, here are the rules," she said, ticking them off on her fingers. "We form a nice, straight line. We stay together at all times. When we get to the park, we'll eat our lunches, then come back here. No running. No roughhousing. If anyone breaks the rules, we come back immediately. Is that understood?"

They listened to every word, expressions dutifully serious as they nodded their understanding. "Yes, ma'am," they said in a reassuring chorus.

Alice figured they would forget everything she'd said the minute they got outdoors, but she refused to let the prospect daunt her. She'd been teaching for several years now. No five-year-old had gotten the better of her yet, not for long, anyway.

"Do all of you have your lunches?" she asked.

Brown bags and lunch boxes were held in the air.

"Then line up, two-by-two. Ricky, I want you in front with Francesca."

Ricky immediately made a face. Francesca was a shy girl who never broke the rules. Maybe she'd be a good influence, Alice thought optimistically.

With Ricky right where Alice could keep a watchful eye on him, they made their way without incident to the nearby park, which the school used as a playground. As the kids sat at picnic tables and ate their lunches, Alice turned her face up to the sun and let the warmth ease her pounding headache.

She'd barely closed her eyes when she felt a

frantic tug on her arm and heard Francesca's panicked whisper.

"Ms. Newberry, Ricky's gone."

Alice's eyes snapped open and she scanned the park. She caught a glimpse of the errant boy heading straight for the waterfront, which every child knew was off-limits.

"Ricky Foster, get back here right this second!" she shouted at the top of her lungs. She saw his steps falter and shouted again. "This second!"

His shoulders visibly heaved with a sigh and he reluctantly came trotting back. She was there to greet him, hands on hips. "Young man, you know the rules. What were you thinking?"

"The fishing boats just came in. I was going to see if they brought back any fish," he said reasonably. "I told Francesca not to tell, 'cause I was coming right back." He scowled at the tattler. "How come you had to go and blab?"

"Francesca is not the one who made a mistake," Alice informed him as predictable tears welled up in Francesca's eyes. "You know that."

"But it's really cool when the boats come in." He gave her a pleading look. "I think we should *all* go. We could have a lesson on fishing."

Alice considered the request. Five minutes each way and they would still be back in the classroom in time for one last lesson.

And truthfully, it was hard to resist Ricky. If she had trouble ignoring that sweet face and coaxing tone, it was little wonder that the other kids were putty in his hands. Besides, she could remember what it was like when the air finally warmed and spring fever set in. There were too many tempting possibilities around the sea to sit still for long. At their age, she'd been just as bad, always eager to run off to the beach, to feel the sand between her toes and the splash of waves, no matter how cold.

"Why should I reward you for misbehaving?" she asked Ricky, trying to hold out as a matter of principle.

"It's not a reward for me," he said piously. "It would be punishing everybody else if you didn't let us go." He regarded her earnestly. "They don't deserve to be punished."

Alice sighed. "No, they don't. Okay, then, I suppose we can go for a walk to see the boats," she agreed at last. "The key word is *walk*. No running. Is that understood?"

"Yes, ma'am," Ricky said, his head bobbing.

"Class?"

"No running," they echoed dutifully.

Satisfied that she at least had a shot at keeping them under control, she had the children throw away their trash, then line up. They looked like obedient little angels as they waited for permission to start. She knew in her gut what an illusion that was, but she wasn't quite prepared for chaos to erupt so quickly.

Ricky spotted something—Alice had no idea

what—and took off with a shout, his promise to remain with the group forgotten. Three others followed. Francesca immediately burst into tears, while Alice shouted ineffectively at Ricky, then set off in hot pursuit. The remaining kids galloped in her wake, obviously thrilled to have the chance to run at full throttle without fear of disapproval.

As she tried to catch the errant children and their sneaky little leader, Alice wondered where in her life she'd gone so wrong. Was it when she'd decided on this outing? Was it when she'd come back to Widow's Cove? Or had it been years before, when she'd defied her parents just as rebelliously as Ricky had just defied her?

Whenever the beginning, her life was definitely on a downward spiral right this second, and something told her it was about to get a whole lot worse.

A dozen pint-sized kids thundered across the rickety, narrow dock straight toward certain disaster. Patrick Devaney heard their exuberant shouts and looked up just in time to see the leader trip over a loose board and nosedive straight into the freezing, churning water.

Muttering a heartfelt oath, Patrick instinctively dove into the Atlantic after the boy, scooped him up and had him sitting on the edge of the dock before the kid was fully aware of just how close he'd come to drowning. No matter how good a swimmer the kid was, the icy waters could have numbed him in no time, and his skill would have been useless.

Patrick automatically whirled on the woman accompanying the children. "What the *hell* were you thinking?" he demanded heatedly.

Clearly frozen with shock, cheeks flushed, she stared at him, her mouth working. Then, to his complete dismay, she burst into tears. Patrick barely contained a harsh expletive. A near drowning and a blubbering female. The day just got better and better.

Sighing, he jumped onto the deck of his fishing boat—which also happened to be his home at the moment—grabbed a blanket and wrapped it around the shivering boy. He shrugged out of his own soaked flannel shirt and into a dry wool jacket, keeping his gaze steady on the kid and ignoring the ditzy woman responsible for this near disaster.

"You okay, pal?" he asked after a while.

Eyes wide, the boy nodded. "Just cold," he said, his teeth chattering.

"Yeah, it's not exactly a perfect day for a swim," Patrick agreed. The temperature was mild for a midafternoon in April on the coast of Maine, but the ocean was cold enough to chill a beer in a couple of minutes. He knew, because he'd done it more than once lately. The sea was more efficient than a refrigerator. And if the water was that effective on a beer, it wouldn't take much longer than that to disable a boy this kid's size and have him sinking like a rock straight to the bottom. He shuddered just thinking about the tragedy this accident could have become.

The kid watched him warily. "Don't blame Ms. Newberry," he pleaded. "I tripped. It wasn't her fault."

Patrick could have debated the point. Who in their right mind brought a bunch of rambunctious children onto a dock—a clearly marked *private* dock—without sufficient supervision? He scowled once more in the woman's direction, noting that she'd apparently recovered from her bout of tears and was carefully herding the rest of the children back onto dry land. Her soft voice carried out to him as she instructed them firmly to stay put. He could have told her it was a futile command. Children as young as these were inevitably more adventurous than either sensible or obedient. Besides, they outnumbered her, always a risky business when dealing with kids.

"Ms. Newberry's going to be real mad at me," the boy beside him confided gloomily. "She told us not to run. We were supposed to stay together."

Patrick bit back a smile at the futility of that order. "How come you didn't listen?"

" 'Cause I was in a hurry," he replied impatiently.

Patrick understood the logic of that. He also thought he recognized the kid. It was Matt Foster's boy. Matt rushed through life the same way, always at full tilt and without a lick of common sense. "You're Ricky Foster, aren't you?"

"Uh-huh," he said, head bobbing. "How come you know that?"

"Your dad and I went to school together. I'd better call him and tell him what's happened," Patrick said. "You need to get home and into some dry clothes."

"I'll see that he gets home," the woman in charge of the group informed him stiffly.

"You sure you can handle that and keep an eye on the others, too?" Patrick inquired, nodding toward the brood that was already racing off in a dozen different directions.

Muttering a very unladylike oath under her breath, she charged back to shore and rounded up the children for a second time. She looked as if she'd like nothing better than to tie each and every one of them to a hitching post.

Patrick took pity on her and carried the still-shivering Ricky back to join the others. With two adults presenting a united front, maybe they'd have a shot at averting any more disasters.

"Let's take 'em all over to Jess's where they can warm up while you call Matt Foster and get him down here," Patrick suggested. He headed off in that direction without waiting for a reply. A firm grip on his arm jerked him to a stop.

"I don't think a bar is an appropriate place for a group of five-year-olds," she told him.

19

He frowned down at her. "You have a better suggestion?"

"We could take them back to the school. That's what we *should* do," she said, though without much enthusiasm.

Patrick understood her reluctance. The school's principal, Loretta Dowd, had to be a hundred years old by now, and she wasn't known for her leniency. Patrick knew that from his own bitter experience. He'd been every bit as rambunctious as Ricky at his age. There would be hell to pay for this little incident.

"Miss Dowd knows about this outing, then?" he asked, guessing that it had been an impromptu and ill-advised decision. "Permission slips to leave the school grounds are all on file?"

She faltered at that, then sighed. "No," she admitted. "I suppose the bar is a better choice, at least for a few minutes."

"It won't be busy at this time of day," he consoled her. "Most of the fishermen came in hours ago. And you know how Molly likes to cluck over kids."

Jess's had been catering to Widow's Cove fishermen for three generations. Jess had long since passed on, but his granddaughter ran the place with the same disdain for frills. Molly served cold beer and steaming hot chowder, which was all that mattered to her regulars.

When Patrick and Ms. Newberry trooped inside

20

with the children, Molly came out from behind the bar, took one look at the dripping wet Ricky and began clucking over him as predicted.

"What on earth?" Molly asked, then waved off the question. "Never mind. It doesn't matter. I'll have hot chocolate ready in no time." She looked at the teacher and frowned. "Alice, you look terrible. Sit down before you faint on me. Patrick, get the children settled, then for heaven's sakes go and put on some dry pants and a warm shirt under that jacket. I have some of granddad's I can lend you. They're hanging in the pantry on the way to the kitchen. Help yourself. I'll be back in a minute. While I'm in the kitchen, I'll give Matt a call and tell him to get over here to pick up Ricky."

Patrick knew better than to balk openly at one of Molly's orders. She might be his age, but she'd had Jess as an example. She could boss around a fleet of marines without anyone questioning her authority. Besides, one glance at Alice Newberry told him that she was in no condition to take charge. He'd never seen a grown woman look quite so defeated. He had a hunch that today's misadventure was the last straw in a long string of defeats.

He studied her with a bit more sympathy. Every last bit of color had drained out of her delicate, heart-shaped face, and her brown hair had been whipped into a tangle of curls by the wind. The fact that she was making no attempt at all to tame them spoke volumes. Her hands were visibly trembling, as well. If she wasn't in shock, she was darn close to it. He tried not to feel too sorry for her, since she'd brought this mess on herself, but a vulnerable woman could cut through his defenses in a heartbeat. Usually he knew enough to avoid them like the plague. This one had reached out and grabbed him when his defenses were down.

"Sit," he ordered her as he passed by on his way to the bar. Hot chocolate might be great for the kids, but she clearly needed something a lot stronger. He could use the heat from a glass of whiskey himself. He poured two shots and took them back to the table where she was sitting, then slid in opposite her. He wasn't the least bit surprised when she reacted with dismay.

"I can't drink that," she said. "It's the middle of the day and I'm working."

Patrick shrugged. "Suit yourself." He tossed back his own drink, grateful for the fire that shot through his veins. It was only a temporary flash of heat, but it was welcome and would do until he could get home and into his own dry pants.

When he glanced across the table, he found Alice Newberry's solemn gaze locked on him. He had a feeling a man could drown in those golden eyes if he let himself.

"I never thanked you," she said. "You saved Ricky's life. I don't know what I would have done if you hadn't been there."

"You would have jumped in after him," he said, giving her the benefit of the doubt.

She shook her head. "I couldn't," she said in a voice barely above a whisper. "I froze. It's like it happened in slow motion and I couldn't move."

"You only froze for a second," he said, surprised by his reluctance to add to her obvious self-derision. "It all happened very quickly."

"That's all it takes. In a second, everything can change. One minute someone's there and alive and healthy . . . the next, they're gone."

Something told him she was no longer talking about Ricky Foster's misadventure. Something also told him he didn't want to know what demons she was wrestling with. He had more than enough of his own.

Now that he knew who she was, he had a dim recollection of hearing the gossip that the new kindergarten teacher in Widow's Cove was returning home after some personal tragedy. Everyone spoke of it in whispers. Patrick hadn't listened to the details. They hadn't mattered to him. He made it a practice to keep everyone at a distance, to remain completely uninvolved in their lives. It was the one sure way to avoid being betrayed. He had no family in Widow's Cove and few friends. And he liked it that way.

"Yeah, bad stuff happens like that," he said neutrally, in response to Alice's lament. "But all's well that ends well. Ricky will be fine once he gets into some dry clothes. You'll be fine once the shock wears off."

She studied him with surprise. "You didn't sound so philosophical down on the dock. I believe you asked me what the hell I was thinking."

He shrugged. "It seemed like a valid question at the time." Now that the crisis was over, his temper had cooled and his own share in the guilt had crept in.

"It was a perfectly reasonable question," she agreed, surprising him.

"I don't suppose you have a perfectly reasonable answer, do you?"

She nodded. "Actually, I do. The children were getting restless at school. Spring break starts tomorrow. I thought a walk would do them good. The next thing I knew, Ricky spied the last of the fishing boats coming in. He begged to come and see what kind of catch everyone had. He swore to me that he'd stay with the group. Everyone agreed not to run. I took them at their word."

She shrugged and gave Patrick a wry look. "Obviously, I should have known better. Five seconds later, Ricky spied something, who knows what, and forgot all about his promise. He took off, and the next thing I knew they were all off and running. I've been teaching five-year-olds long enough now to have anticipated something like that."

"Maybe so, but you couldn't anticipate Ricky tripping," Patrick replied, then conceded with reluctance, "Besides, the fault's as much mine as yours. I've known that board was loose since I bought the dock, but I keep forgetting to pick up some nails when I'm at the hardware store. I've gotten so used to it, I just walk around it. Nobody else comes down that way. That dock's supposed to be private."

She regarded him with surprise. "In Widow's Cove?"

Patrick chafed under the hint of disapproval he thought he heard. "I bought and paid for it. Why shouldn't I put up No Trespassing signs?"

"It's just unusual in a friendly town like this," she said. "Most people don't see the need."

"I don't like being bothered." No need to explain that the signs were meant as a deterrent for certain specific people, Patrick thought. If they kept everyone else away, too, so much the better.

He glanced up and caught sight of Matt Foster coming through the door. "Ricky's dad's here," he told Alice, making no attempt to hide his relief. "I'll speak to him and tell him what happened, then I'll be getting back to my boat."

"I'll explain," Alice insisted, her chin jutting up with determination as she slid from the booth. "It's my responsibility."

"Whatever," he said with a shrug. "One word of advice, though. Next time you think about taking your class for a stroll, think again. Either that or keep 'em away from the docks."

There was a surprising flash of temper in her eyes at the order he'd clumsily tried to disguise as advice. For an instant Patrick thought she was going to address him with another burst of unladylike profanity, but one glance at the children silenced her. Discretion didn't dim the sparks in her eyes, nor did it quiet her tongue. She looked him straight in the eye and said, "If the occasion ever arises again, I'll certainly consider your point of view, Mr. Devaney."

The fact that her meek tone was counterpointed by sparks of barely restrained annoyance pretty much ruined the polite effect he was sure she intended. Patrick shook his head.

"Just keep 'em away from my dock, then," he said, dropping all pretenses. "And that's not a simple request, Ms. Newberry. That's an order."

She was still sputtering indignantly when he spoke to Matt and then walked out the door.

Something about that little display of temper got to him, made his blood heat in a way it hadn't for a while. He savored the sensation for a moment, then deliberately dismissed it. All it proved was that he needed to keep his distance from Alice Newberry. If a woman could get under his skin with a flash of temper, then he'd been seriously deprived of female companionship for far too long. He suspected the kindergarten teacher with the tragic past and the vulnerable expression was the last woman on earth he should choose to change that.

Chapter Two

The minute he'd taken a hot shower and changed into dry clothes, Patrick headed for the hardware store in downtown Widow's Cove. Today's near tragedy had been just the wake-up call he needed to repair the dock once and for all.

He'd let too many things slip the past few years, not caring about anything more than the hours at sea, the size of his catch and a cold beer at the end of a hard day. Ricky Foster's plunge into the ocean had shocked him back to reality. Unless he planned to move to some uninhabited island, Patrick couldn't keep the world at bay forever. And since he couldn't, he'd better be prepared for the intrusions, if only to make sure that no one could sue his butt off.

That cynical response aside, he had another pressing issue to consider—his disturbing reaction to Alice Newberry. He could fix the dock to keep some other kid from tripping, but he wasn't nearly as sure how to go about protecting himself from the likes of the teacher.

Maybe Molly would give him some pointers on that score. The two women were obviously acquainted. He figured, knowing Molly, that asking questions would stir up a hornet's nest, but that was still better than risking another encounter when Alice Newberry could catch him off guard and get to him with those big golden eyes of hers.

At the old-fashioned hardware store, which was stacked from floor to ceiling with every size nut and bolt imaginable, along with tools for everything from fixing a leak to building a mansion, Patrick picked out the nails he needed to repair the dock, added some treated lumber to replace the boards that were warped beyond repair, then went up to the counter.

Caleb Jenkins, who'd taken over the store from his father fifty years ago and modernized very little beyond the selection of merchandise, gave him a nod and what passed for a smile. "Figured you'd be in," he said.

"Oh?"

"Heard what happened on the dock," Caleb explained. "Board's been loose since Red Foley bought that dock thirty years ago. Told him a hundred times, the dang thing was a danger. Would've told you the same thing, if you'd come in here before now, but you've been making yourself scarce since you moved over here from your folks' place."

Patrick's grin faltered at the mention of his parents, but that was a discussion he didn't intend to have—not with Caleb Jenkins, not with anyone. He'd written his folks off, and the reasons were his business and his alone. The fact that they were less than thirty miles away meant he was bound to run into people who knew them from time to time. It didn't mean he had to discuss his personal business.

Instead he focused on the rest of Caleb's comment. "Doubt I'd have listened any better than Red," he told the old man.

"Probably not." Caleb shook his head. "You get old and finally know a thing or two and nobody wants to listen. Heard the boy's okay, though."

"Just wet and scared," Patrick confirmed. "I imagine Matt will have quite a bit to say to him."

"Doubtful. Matt never had a lick of sense. Always in a hurry, Matt was. Boy's the same way," he said, confirming Patrick's previous thought that like father, like son.

"You have a point," Patrick agreed.

"Matt lived to tell a tale or two about his narrow escapes. I imagine his son will, too."

"Hope so," Patrick said. He peeled off the money to pay for the nails and lumber, anxious to get home, finish the needed work and put this day behind him.

Caleb gave him a sly look as he handed back the receipt. "Hear Alice Newberry took what happened real hard."

"She was upset, but she'll get over it. After all, there was no real harm done."

"Doubt Loretta will see it that way," Caleb said, shaking his head. "How that woman ended up principal of a school is beyond me. She never did understand kids. You gotta let 'em explore and discover things for themselves. They're bound to make a few mistakes along the way, but that's just part of living, don't you think?"

Patrick hadn't given the topic much thought, since he had no kids of his own and didn't intend to. "Makes sense to me," he said, mostly to end the conversation. He had a hunch Caleb was leading up to something Patrick didn't want to hear.

Unfortunately, Caleb wasn't the least bit daunted. "Maybe you ought to go by the school and have a word with Loretta."

Patrick gave him a hard look. "Me? Why should I get involved?"

"You are involved," Caleb pointed out. "The boy fell off your dock. Besides, a man ought to be willing to help out a woman when she needs looking after. That's the way of the world."

The old-fashioned world, maybe, Patrick thought. He wasn't sure he had any reason to get involved in Alice Newberry's salvation. As well, he had a hunch she could stand up for herself just fine. Aside from that brief display of tears, which he attributed to shock, she hadn't hesitated to speak her mind to him. She seemed to have some sort of fixation on personal accountability, too. He doubted she would appreciate him running to her rescue.

"I'll think about it," he told Caleb.

"Not much of a gentleman if you don't," the old man said, his tone chiding.

"If I hear Ms. Newberry needs any help, I'll talk to Loretta," he promised.

"That'll do, I suppose," Caleb said, looking disappointed.

"I imagine you'd go rushing over to the school right now," Patrick said, feeling the weight of the subtle pressure.

Caleb's expression brightened at once. "There you go. Best to nip this sort of thing in the bud. Be sure to give Loretta my regards."

"I never said I was going to the school," Patrick pointed out.

"Of course you are. It's ten minutes away. Won't take you but a couple of minutes to put things right with Loretta, and you can be back on that dock of yours in no time. You'll have done a good deed."

"I thought diving in the freezing ocean *was* my good deed," Patrick grumbled.

"One of 'em," Caleb agreed. "A smart man knows he needs a lot of 'em on the ledger before the day comes when he faces Saint Peter."

Patrick sighed heavily. "I'll keep that in mind."

He noticed that Caleb was looking mighty pleased with himself as he watched Patrick gather up his purchases. Just what he needed in his life . . . a nosy old man who thought he had a right to be Patrick's conscience.

Nevertheless, he drove to the school, then stalked through the halls that still smelled exactly as they had twenty years ago—of chalk, a strong

31

pine-scented cleanser, peanut butter sandwiches and smelly sneakers. He followed the all-too-familiar path directly to the principal's office and hammered on the door, determined for once not to let Loretta Dowd intimidate him. He was all grown-up and beyond her authority now.

"Come in," a tart voice snapped.

Patrick entered and faced Loretta Dowd with her flashing black eyes and steel-gray bun. He promptly felt as if he were six years old again, and in trouble for the tenth time in one day.

"You!" she said. "I might have known. There's no need to break my door down, Patrick Devaney. My hearing's still perfectly fine."

He winced at her censure. "Yes, ma'am."

"I imagine you're here to tell me that it wasn't Alice's fault that Ricky Foster fell off your dock."

Patrick nodded.

"Did you take him from his classroom to the waterfront?"

Patrick barely resisted the desire to squirm as he had as a boy under that unflinching gaze. "No."

"Did you lose control of him?"

"No."

"Then I don't see how this is your fault," she said. "You may go now."

Patrick started to leave, then realized what she hadn't said. He turned back and peered at her. "You're not firing Ms. Newberry, are you?"

32

She frowned at the question. "Don't be ridiculous. She's a fine teacher. She just happened to make a bad decision today. Spring makes a lot of people do crazy things. We've addressed it. It won't happen again."

Thank the Lord for that, Patrick thought. "Okay, then," he said.

He turned to leave, but Mrs. Dowd spoke his name sharply.

"Yes, ma'am?" He noticed with some surprise that there was a twinkle in her eyes.

"It was very gallant of you to roar in here in an attempt to protect Ms. Newberry. You've turned into a fine young man."

Warmth flooded through him at the undeserved compliment. "I imagine there are quite a few who'd argue that point," he said, "but thanks for saying it, just the same."

"If you're referring to your parents, I think you know better."

Patrick stiffened. "I don't discuss my parents."

"Perhaps you should. Better yet, you should be talking to them. And to your brother."

"They're in my past," he told her, not the least bit surprised that she felt she had a right to meddle in his life but resentful of it just the same.

"Not as long as there's breath in any of you," she told him, her tone surprisingly gentle. "One phone call would put an end to their heartache." She leveled her gaze straight at him. "And to yours."

"My heart's just fine, thanks all the same, and I didn't come here to get a lecture from you," he said. "I left grade school a long time ago."

"But you haven't outgrown the need for a friendly nudge from someone older and wiser, have you?" she chided.

It was the second time in less than an hour that someone in town had seen fit to pull rank on Patrick. It was Caleb's push that had gotten him over here, and for what? He hadn't done a thing to help Alice Newberry, and he'd gotten another lecture on his own life in the bargain.

"Forgive me for saying this, Mrs. Dowd, but in this case you don't know what you're talking about."

"I know enough to recognize a miserable man when I see one standing in front of me," she said. "You won't be truly happy until you settle this."

"Maybe it can't be settled and maybe I don't care about being truly happy," Patrick retorted. "Maybe all I care about is being left alone."

That said, he whirled around and left the school, regretting that he'd ever let Caleb talk him into coming over here in the first place. Some days a man would be smart to listen to his own counsel and no one else's.

Alice had never been so humiliated and embarrassed in her life. Of all the boneheaded things she could have done . . . not only had she lost control of her students and let one of them nearly drown, she had done it in front of Patrick Devaney.

Everyone in Widow's Cove knew that Patrick had turned into a virtual recluse. He lived on that fishing boat of his, ate his meals at Jess's and, for all Alice knew, drank himself into oblivion there every night as well. What no one knew was why, not the details, anyway. There had been some sort of rift with his parents, that much was known. He'd left his home, about thirty miles away, and moved to Widow's Cove. That thirty miles might as well have been thirty thousand. From what she'd heard, none of them had bridged the distance.

Alice almost hadn't recognized Patrick when he'd emerged from the ocean dripping wet and mad as the dickens. His hair was too long and stubble shadowed his cheeks. He looked just a little disreputable and more than a little dangerous, especially with his intense blue eyes shooting angry sparks.

Alice remembered a very different Patrick from high school. Although she'd been two years older, everyone at the county high school located here in town knew each other at least by sight. Even as a sophomore, Patrick had been the flirtatious, wildly popular, star football player; his twin brother, Daniel, the captain of the team. The two of them had been inseparable. Now they barely spoke and tried to avoid crossing paths. No one understood that, either.

Alice hadn't been surprised that Patrick hadn't remembered her. Not only had she been older, but in high school she'd kept her head buried in her books. She'd been determined to go to college, to break the pattern of all the women in her family, going back generations, who'd married seafaring men, borne their children and lived in fear each time a violent storm approached the coast.

Too many of those men had been lost at sea. Too many of the wives had raised their children alone, living a hand-to-mouth existence because they'd had no skills of their own to fall back on. It had been such a bitter irony that her own father had been lost to that same sea—not in a boat, but in a car—and that he'd taken Alice's mother to her death with him.

Alice could still recall the heated exchange when she'd told her parents of her plans. They'd both thought she was casting aspersions on their choices, that by wanting more she was being ungrateful for the life they'd struggled to give her.

Maybe that was why, even when Patrick had been lambasting her for what had happened this afternoon, Alice had felt a strange sort of kinship with him. She knew all about family rifts and unhealed wounds. He, at least, still had time to heal his before it was too late. Maybe they'd met so that she could pass along the message she'd learned, assuming they ever crossed paths again.

She was about to leave school for the day when the screechy public address system in her room came on with a burst of static. "Alice, my office now, please," Mrs. Dowd said in her usual tart manner.

Alice sighed. She thought they'd already been over today's transgression and moved on. Apparently she'd been wrong. Maybe Matt Foster had called and made an issue of what had happened to Ricky. Maybe he'd forced the principal's hand.

Gathering her things, she headed for the office, filled with a sense of dread. Even though living in Widow's Cove hadn't yet brought her the peace she'd hoped for, she didn't want to leave, and that was exactly what being fired would mean, since there was no other kindergarten class for miles and miles along this remote stretch of coast.

She tapped lightly on the principal's door, then walked in when the woman's sharp tone summoned her.

"There's something I thought you should know before you go off on break for the next week," Loretta Dowd said, a surprising hint of a smile on her usually stern lips.

"Yes?"

"Patrick Devaney was here."

Alice stared at her. Had he come to complain that she wasn't responsible, that she had no business being in charge of a classroom full of children?

"Why?" she asked, barely able to squeeze the word out past the sudden lump in her throat.

"I believe he wanted to save your job if it was in jeopardy. I told him it wasn't, but I think the attempt spoke very well of him, don't you?"

Alice nodded, too shocked for words. Patrick had come rushing to her rescue? He'd been furious with her. Obviously someone was behind it. Molly perhaps. Of course, as fast as news spread in Widow's Cove, it could have been anyone. Few people in town hesitated to share their opinions of right and wrong under the guise of being helpful. Someone had definitely given him a nudge, no question about it.

"Be sure to thank him when you see him," the principal said, a twinkle in her eyes.

"I hadn't planned—"

"The man dove into the icy water to save one of your students," Mrs. Dowd said, cutting her off. "And then he came charging into my office to save you. Don't you think the least you can do would be to take him some homemade soup as an expression of gratitude?"

Alice stared at her, trying to process this bit of advice. If she wasn't mistaken, Loretta Dowd was matchmaking. "What are you up to?" she asked, stunned that the woman even had an interest in Alice's love life.

The principal drew herself up and gave Alice one of her most daunting looks. "I am not up to anything," she declared fiercely, but the indignation came too late.

Alice could see quite clearly now that Loretta Dowd was a complete and total fraud. She was not the strict, unfeeling disciplinarian everyone feared. She had a heart.

"If you can't make soup, I made a fresh pot of chowder this morning," the principal added.

Alice grinned. "I can make soup. In fact, I made some last night and there's plenty left. I baked several loaves of bread, too."

"Well then, what are you standing around here for?" Mrs. Dowd said with her familiar exasperation. "Get on over to that boy's boat before he catches his death of cold."

"Yes, ma'am."

Relieved to have an excuse to force her to do what she'd been half wanting to do, anyway, Alice walked to her house, filled a container with some of her homemade beef vegetable soup, added a loaf of her home-baked bread to the basket, and headed right back to Patrick Devaney's private, No Trespassing dock.

Once there, she took a certain perverse pleasure in pushing open the flimsy gate and making a lot of noise as she approached his trawler. She wasn't the least bit surprised when he emerged from below deck with a scowl already firmly in place.

"Which part of 'stay away' didn't you understand?" he inquired, leaping gracefully onto the dock and blocking her way.

"I figured it didn't apply to me, since I come bearing gifts," she said cheerfully, holding out the soup and bread as she took note of the fact that there were several new boards in place underfoot. "You never mentioned the fact that you were in that freezing ocean because of me—"

"Because of Ricky," he corrected.

She shrugged at the distinction. "I thought some hot soup might ward off a chill. I don't want it on my conscience if you get sick because of what happened. Besides, I need to thank you for going to see Mrs. Dowd this afternoon. She was impressed."

His mouth curved into an arrogant grin that made her heart do an unexpected flip.

"I don't get sick," he informed her. "And I didn't go by the school to impress Loretta Dowd."

"Which makes it all the more fascinating that you did," she replied. "As for your general state of good health, having some nutritious soup won't hurt."

"You casting aspersions on Molly's chowder?"

"Hardly, but you must be tired of that by now."

The grin faded. "Meaning?"

She faltered. She hadn't meant to admit that she knew anything about his habits. "She says you're there a lot, that's all."

"You asked about me?" He didn't even attempt to hide his surprise.

The arrogant tilt to his mouth returned, and Alice saw a faint hint of the charming boy he'd once been. She wasn't here to inflate his already well-developed ego, though. "I most certainly did not," she said. "Molly tends to volunteer information she thinks will prove helpful."

He sighed at that. "Yeah. I keep talking to her about that. She seems to think she can save me from myself if she gets enough people pestering me."

"What do you think?" Alice asked curiously.

"That I don't need saving."

She laughed. "I keep telling her the same thing. It hasn't stopped her yet. Now we've both got Loretta Dowd meddling in our lives. She's the one who insisted on the soup. We're probably doomed."

"Don't remind me," he said. "I imagine Mrs. Dowd will want to know exactly how polite I was when you came over here. She and Caleb Jenkins will probably compare notes."

"How on earth did Caleb get involved in this?" Alice asked.

"He thought I should speak to Mrs. Dowd on your behalf."

"Ah, that explains the trip to the school. I guessed it wasn't your idea."

"Oh, I suppose I would have come around to it sooner or later on my own," he claimed. "The point is, there are any number of fascinated bystanders in this town. I'll hear about it if I act ungrateful and send you away." He pushed off from the railing and held out his hand. "You want to come aboard and share a bowl of that soup? Looks to me like there's plenty for two."

Alice hesitated. Wasn't this the real reason she'd come, to see if she and Patrick Devaney had as much in common as it seemed? Wasn't she here because of that feeling of kinship that had sparked to life in her earlier?

"Are you sure?" she asked. "You don't seem very receptive to company." She nodded toward the No Trespassing sign.

He gave her a steady, intense look. "It doesn't apply to invited guests, and where you're concerned, I'm not sure of anything," he said in a way that sent a surprising shiver of awareness racing over her.

"Want to wait till you are?" she asked, startled by the teasing note in her own voice. She almost sounded as if she were flirting with him. Of course, it had been a long time, so maybe she wasn't being as obvious as she thought.

"Hell, no," he said, grinning. "I've gotten used to living dangerously."

Alice laughed, then reached out to accept his outstretched hand as she stepped onboard. She noted that unlike the previously decrepit dock, the boat was spotless and in excellent repair. Every piece of chrome and wood had been polished to a soft sheen.

Fishing nets were piled neatly. Apparently Patrick Devaney used the time he didn't spend socializing or shaving to pay close attention to his surroundings.

Below deck in the small cabin, it was the same. The table was clear except for the half-filled coffee cup from which he'd apparently been drinking. The bed a few feet away was neatly made, the sheets crisp and clean, a navy-blue blanket folded precisely at the foot of the bed.

Moving past her in the tight space, Patrick took a pot from a cupboard, poured the soup into it and set it on the small two-burner stove, then retrieved two bowls and spoons from the same cupboard. Alice was all too aware of the way he filled the cramped quarters, of the width of his shoulders, of the narrowness of his hips. He'd filled in since his football-playing days, but he was definitely still in shape. It was the first time in ages she'd recognized the powerful effect pure masculinity could have on her.

From the moment she'd lost her parents, nearly a year ago, she'd gone into an emotional limbo. She let no one or nothing touch her. She even kept a barrier up between herself and her students, or at least she had until Ricky Foster had scared the living daylights out of her this afternoon. Nothing had rattled her so badly since the night the police had called to tell her that her parents had driven off that road they'd traveled a thousand times in all kinds of weather.

Don't go there, she thought, forcing her attention back to the present. One appreciative, surreptitious glance at Patrick's backside as he bent to retrieve something from the tiny refrigerator did the trick. It was all she could do not to sigh audibly at the sight.

Don't go there, either, she told herself very firmly. She was here for penance and for soup. Nothing more. A peek at Patrick Devaney sent another little shock of awareness through her and proved otherwise.

Oh, well, there was certainly no harm in looking, she decided as she sat back and enjoyed the view. Even a woman living in a self-imposed state of celibacy had the right to her fantasies, and any fantasy involving Patrick Devaney should definitely not be dismissed too readily.

Chapter Three

Patrick wasn't sure what had possessed him to invite Alice Newberry aboard the *Katie G.*, a boat he'd named for his mother as a constant reminder that people weren't to be trusted. For eighteen years he'd considered his mother to be the most admirable woman he'd ever known. Now, each time he caught a glimpse of the name painted on the bow of the boat, it served as a reminder that everyone had secrets and that everyone was capable of duplicity. It was a cynical attitude, but experience had taught him it was a valid one.

Maybe he'd invited Alice to join him because he was getting sick of his own lousy company. Or maybe it was because he had a gut instinct that she'd learned the same bitter lesson about humanity's lack of trustworthiness. Not that he planned to commiserate. He just figured she was probably no more anxious than he was to start something that was destined to end badly, the way all relationships inevitably did.

Oddly enough, for all that they'd had going against them, his own parents were still together. He supposed there was some sort of perverse love at work, if it could survive what they'd done to their own family. Funny how for so many years he'd thought how lucky he was to have had parents who'd stayed together, parents who preached about steadfastness and commitment and set an example for their sons.

He and Daniel had had a lot of friends whose parents were divorced, kids who'd envied them for their ideal home. Not that Patrick or Daniel had shared the illusion that everything was wonderful in the Devaney household. There were arguments—plenty of them, in fact—mostly conducted in whispers and behind closed doors. And there were undercurrents they'd never understood—an occasional expression of inexplicable sorrow on their mother's face, an occasional hint of resentment in their father's eyes—just enough to make him and Daniel wonder if things were as perfect as they wanted to believe.

In general, though, he and Daniel had had a good life. There had been a lot of love showered on them, love that in retrospect he could see was meant to make up for the love their parents could no longer give to their other sons. There had been tough times financially, but they'd never gone to bed hungry or doubting that they were loved. And in later years, his father had settled into a good-paying job as a commercial fisherman, working not for himself but for some conglomerate that guaranteed a paycheck, even when the catches weren't up to par. After that, things had been even better. There were no more arguments over rent and grocery money.

He and Daniel had been eighteen before they'd

46

discovered the truth, and then all of those whispered fights and sad looks had finally made sense. Not that their parents had confessed to anything in a sudden flash of conscience. No, the truth had been left for Patrick and Daniel to discover by accident.

Daniel had been digging around in an old trunk in the attic, hoping to use it to haul his belongings away to college, when he'd stumbled on an envelope of yellowing photos, buried beneath some old clothes. It was apparent in a heartbeat that the envelope was something they'd never been meant to see.

Patrick still remembered that day as if it were yesterday. If he let himself, he could feel the oppressive heat, smell the dust that swirled as Daniel disturbed memories too long untouched. To this day, if Patrick walked into a room that had been closed up too long, the musty scent of it disturbed him. It was why he'd chosen to live here, on his boat, where the salt air breezes held no memories.

He remembered Daniel shouting for him to come upstairs, remembered the confused expression on his twin's face as he'd sifted through the stack of photographs. When Patrick had climbed the ladder into the attic, Daniel looked stunned. Silently, he held out the pictures, his hand trembling.

"Look at them," he commanded, when Patrick's gaze stayed on him rather than the photos.

"Looks like some old pictures," Patrick had said, barely sparing them a glance, far more concerned about his brother's odd expression.

"*Look* at them," his brother had repeated impatiently.

The sense of urgency had finally gotten through to Patrick, and he'd studied the first picture. It was of a toddler with coal-black hair and a happy smile racing toward the camera at full throttle. He was a blur of motion. Patrick had blinked at the image, thoroughly confused about what Daniel had seen that had him so obviously upset. "What? Do you think it's Dad?"

Daniel shook his head. "Look again. That's Dad in the background."

"Okay," Patrick said slowly, still not sure what Daniel was getting at. "Then it has to be one of us."

"I don't think so. Look at the rest of the pictures."

Slowly, Patrick had worked his way through the photos, several dozen in all, apparently spanning a period of years. His mom was in some of them, his father in more. But there were happy, smiling boys in each one. That first toddler, then another who was his spitting image, then three, and finally five, two of them babies, evidently twins.

Patrick's hand shook as he studied the last set of pictures. Finally, almost as distressed and definitely as confused as Daniel, he dragged his gaze away and stared at his brother. "My God, what do you think it means? Those babies, do you think that's you and me?"

"Who else could it be?" Daniel had asked. "There are no other twins on either side of the family, at least none that we know of. Come to think of it, though, what do we really know about our family? Have you ever heard one word about our grandparents, about any aunts or uncles?"

"No."

"That should have told us something. It's as if we're some insular little group that sprang on the world with absolutely no connections to anyone else on earth."

"Don't you think you're being overly dramatic?" Patrick asked.

"Look at the damn pictures and tell me again that I'm being too dramatic," Daniel shouted back at him.

Patrick's gaze had automatically gone to the top photo, the one of five little dark-haired boys. "Who do you suppose they are?"

"I don't even want to think about it," Daniel said, clearly shaken to his core by the implications.

"We have to ask Mom and Dad. You know that," Patrick told him, feeling sick. "We can't leave it alone."

"Why not? Obviously, it's something they don't want to talk about," Daniel argued, far too eager to stick his head right back in the sand.

It had always been that way. Patrick liked to confront things, to lay all the cards on the table, no matter what the consequences. Daniel liked peace at any cost. He'd been the perfect team captain on their high school football squad, because he had no ego, because he could smooth over the competitive streaks and keep the team functioning as a unit.

"It doesn't matter what they want," Patrick had all but shouted, as angered now as Daniel had been a moment earlier. "If those boys are related to us, if they're our *brothers,* we have a right to know. We need to know what happened to them. Did they die? Why haven't we ever heard about them? Kids don't just vanish into thin air."

"Maybe they're cousins or something," Daniel said, seeking a less volatile explanation. It was as if he couldn't bear to even consider the hard questions, much less the answers.

"Then why haven't we seen them in years?" Patrick wasn't about to let their folks off the hook . . . or Daniel, for that matter. This was too huge to ignore. And it could explain so many things, little things and big ones, that had never made any sense. "You said it yourself, the folks have never once mentioned any other relatives."

Even as he spoke, he searched his memory, trying to find the faintest recollection of having big brothers, but nothing came to him. Shouldn't he have remembered on some subconscious level at least? He scanned the pictures again, hoping to

50

trigger something. On his third try, he noticed the background.

"Daniel, where do you think these were taken?" he asked, puzzled by what he saw.

"Around here, I guess. It's where we've always lived."

"Is it?" Patrick asked, studying the buildings in the photos. "Have you ever noticed a skyscraper in Widow's Cove?"

Daniel reached for the photo. "Let me see that." He studied it intently. "Boston? Could it be Boston?"

Patrick shrugged. "I don't know, I've never been to Boston. You went there with some friends last Christmas. Does it look familiar to you?"

"I honestly don't know, but if it is Boston, why haven't Mom and Dad ever mentioned that we took a trip there?"

"Or lived there?" Patrick added. "We have to ask, Daniel. If you won't, then I will."

Patrick remembered the inevitable confrontation with their parents as if it had taken place only yesterday. He'd been the one to put the photos on the kitchen table in front of their mother. He'd tried to remain immune to her shocked gasp of recognition, but it had cut right through him. That gasp was as much of an admission as any words would have been, and it had stripped away every shred of respect he'd ever felt for her. In a heartbeat, she went from beloved mother to complete stranger.

51

"What the hell have you two been doing digging around in the attic?" his father had shouted, making a grab for the pictures. "There are things up there that are none of your business."

But all of Connor Devaney's blustery anger and Kathleen's silent tears hadn't cut through Patrick's determination to get at the truth. He'd finally gotten them to admit that those three boys were their sons, sons they had abandoned years before when they'd brought Patrick and Daniel to Maine.

"And you've never seen them again?" he'd asked, shocked at the confirmation of something he'd suspected but hadn't wanted to believe. "You have no idea what happened to them?"

"We made sure someone would look after them, then we made a clean break," his father said defensively. He looked at his wife as if daring her to contradict him. "It was for the best."

"What do you mean, you made sure someone would look after them? Did you arrange an adoption?"

"We made a call to Social Services," his father said.

"They said someone would go right out, that the boys would be taken care of," his mother said, as if that made everything all right.

Even as he'd heard the words, Patrick hadn't wanted to believe them. How could these two people he'd loved, people who'd loved him, have been so cold, so irresponsible? What kind of person thought that making a phone call to the authorities made up for taking care of their own children? What parents walked away from their children without making any attempt to *assure beyond any doubt* that they were in good hands? What kind of people chose one child over another and then pretended for years that their family of four was complete? My God, his whole life had been one lie after another.

Patrick had been overwhelmed with guilt over having been chosen, while three little boys—his own brothers—had been abandoned.

"How old were they?" he asked, nearly choking on the question.

"What difference does it make?" his father asked.

"How old?" Patrick repeated.

"Nine, seven and four," his mother confessed in a voice barely above a whisper. Tears tracked down her cheeks, and she suddenly looked older.

"My God!" Patrick had shoved away from the kitchen table, barely resisting the desire to break things, to shatter dishes the way his illusions had been shattered.

"Let us explain," his mother had begged.

"We don't owe them an explanation," his father had shouted over her. "We did what we had to do. We've given the two of them a good life. That's what we owed them. They've no right to question our decision."

Patrick hadn't been able to silence all the questions still churning inside him. "What about what you owed your other sons?" he had asked, feeling dead inside. "Did you ever once think about them? My God, what were you thinking?"

He hadn't waited for answers. He'd known none would be forthcoming, not with his mother in tears and his father stubbornly digging in his heels. Besides, the answers didn't really matter. There was no justification for what they'd done. He'd whirled around and left the house that night, taking nothing with him, wanting nothing from people capable of doing such a thing. It was the last time he'd seen or spoken to either one of his parents.

Daniel had found him a week later, drunk on the waterfront in Widow's Cove. He'd tried for hours to convince Patrick to come home.

"I don't have a home," Patrick had told him, meaning it. "Why should I have one, when our brothers never did?"

"You don't know that," Daniel had argued. "It's possible they've had good lives with wonderful families."

"Possible?" he'd scoffed. "Separated from us? Maybe even separated from each other? And that's good enough to satisfy you? You're as bad as they are. The Devaneys are a real piece of work. With genes like ours, the world is doomed."

"Stop it," Daniel ordered, looking miserable. "You don't know the whole story."

Patrick had looked his brother in the eye, momentarily wondering if he'd learned things that had been kept from Patrick. "Do you?"

"No, but—"

"I don't want to hear your phony excuses, then. Leave me alone, Daniel. Go on off to college. Live your life. Pretend that none of this ever happened. I can't. I'll never go back there."

He'd watched his brother walk away and suffered a moment's regret for the years of closeness lost, but he'd pushed it aside and made up his mind that he would spend the rest of his life living down the Devaney name. Maybe what that meant wasn't public knowledge, but he would live with the shame just the same.

That was the last time he'd gotten drunk, the last day he'd wandered idly. He'd gotten a job on a fishing boat and started saving until he'd been able to afford his own trawler. His needs were simple—peace and quiet, an occasional beer, the infrequent companionship of a woman who wasn't looking for a future. He tried with everything in him to be a decent man, but he feared that as Connor and Kathleen's son, he was a lost cause.

He spent a lot of lonely nights trying like the very dickens not to think about the three older brothers who'd been left behind years ago. He'd thought about hunting for them, then dismissed the notion. Why the hell would they care about a brother who'd been given everything, while they'd gotten nothing?

He heard about his folks from time to time. Widow's Cove wasn't that far from home, after all. And in the past twenty-four hours, he'd heard far too many references to his family, first from Caleb Jenkins, then from Loretta Dowd. As for Daniel, Patrick knew his brother was in Portland much of the time, working, ironically, as a child advocate with the courts. Daniel had found his own, less-rebellious way of coping with what their parents had done.

Patrick sighed at the memories crashing over him tonight. He concentrated harder on the soup he was heating, then ladling into bowls, on the crusty loaf of homemade bread he sliced and set on the table with a tub of margarine.

Over the past few years of self-imposed isolation, Patrick had lost his knack for polite chitchat, but he quickly discovered that tonight it didn't matter. Alice was a grand master. From the moment he sat down opposite her, his presence at the table seemed to loosen her tongue. Maybe it came from spending all day talking to a bunch of rowdy five-year-olds, trying desperately to hold their attention. She regaled Patrick with stories that kept him chuckling and filled the silence better than the TV he usually kept on as background noise. In his day, Ricky Foster would obviously have been labeled a teacher's pet, because his name popped up in the conversation time and again. Alice clearly had a soft spot for the boy.

"Then today wasn't Ricky's first act of rebellion?" he asked when she'd described another occasion on which the boy had gotten the better of her.

"Heavens, no. I'm telling you that boy will be president someday." She shrugged. "Or possibly a convicted felon. It depends on which way his talents for leadership and conning people take him."

"His daddy always lacked the ambition for either one," Patrick said. "I suppose in retrospect a case could be made that Matt had attention-deficit disorder. He couldn't sit still to save his soul. Maybe that's Ricky's problem, too."

Alice regarded him with surprise. "You know about ADHD?"

Patrick leaned closer, then lowered his voice to a whisper. "Why? Is it a secret?"

She blushed prettily. "No, it is not a secret. I just didn't expect . . ." Obvious embarrassment turned her cheeks a deeper shade of pink as her words trailed off in midsentence.

"Didn't expect a fisherman to know anything about it?" he asked, trying not to be offended.

"I'm sorry. That was stupid of me."

"Making assumptions about people is usually the first step toward getting it totally wrong," he replied. Then, because he couldn't resist teasing her, he added, "For instance, right now I am trying really, really hard not to assume that you're here because you want to seduce me."

The color staining her cheeks turned a fiery red. "I see your point. And in case there's any doubt, you would definitely be mistaken about my intentions."

Something about the hitch in her voice told him he wasn't nearly as far off the mark as she wanted him to believe. "Is that so?" he asked, tucking a finger under her chin and forcing her gaze to meet his.

"I came to thank you for saving Ricky," she insisted. She swallowed hard as he traced the outline of her jaw. "And for going to see Mrs. Dowd."

"I'm sure you believe that," he agreed, noting the jump in the pulse at the base of her throat when he ran his thumb lightly across her lower lip.

"Because it's true," she said.

Patrick deliberately lowered his hand and sat back, noting the sudden confusion in her eyes. He shrugged. "Sorry, then. My mistake."

Confusion gave way to another one of those quick flashes of anger that had stirred him earlier in the day.

"That sort of teasing is totally inappropriate, Mr. Devaney," she said in a tone she probably used when correcting a rambunctious five-year-old.

Patrick imagined it had the same effect on Ricky Foster that it had on him. It made him want to test her.

He stood up, picked up his empty soup bowl, then reached for hers. He clasped one hand on her shoulder as he leaned in close, let his breath fan against her cheek, then touched her delicate ear-lobe with the tip of his tongue. She jumped as if she'd been burned.

"Mr. Devaney!"

Patrick laughed at the breathless protest. "Sorry," he apologized, perfectly aware that he didn't sound particularly repentant. Probably because he wasn't.

She frowned at him. "No, you're not. You're not the least bit sorry."

"Maybe a little," he insisted, then ruined it by adding, "But only because I didn't go for a kiss. Something tells me I'm going to regret that later tonight when I'm lying all alone in my bed."

"You would have regretted it more if you'd gone for it," she assured him, drawing herself up in an attempt to look suitably intimidating. "I know a few moves that could have put you on the floor."

He caught her gaze and held it, barely resisting the urge to laugh again. "I'll bet you do," he said quietly.

"Mr. Devaney . . ."

"Since we're old schoolmates, I think you can call me Patrick," he said.

"Maybe the informality is a bad idea," she suggested. "You tend to take liberties as it is."

He did laugh again then. "Darlin', when I really

59

want to take liberties with you, you'll know it." His let his gaze travel over her slowly. "And you'll be ready for it."

"Is that some sort of a dare?"

"Do you want it to be?"

"No, of course not." She shook her head. "I really don't know what to make of you. I expected you to be more . . ."

"Difficult," Patrick supplied.

"Distant," she corrected.

"Ah, yes. Well, there's still a little life left in the hermit. You'd do well to remember that, before you come knocking on my door again."

"I won't be back," she said emphatically.

"You think soup and bread are sufficient thanks for me putting my life on the line to bail you out of a jam?" he asked.

"Absolutely," she said. "And your life was never on the line."

"That water was damn cold," he insisted.

"And you were in and out of it in ten seconds flat."

He gestured toward the outside. "You want to dive in and see how long ten seconds becomes when you hit those icy waves?"

She shuddered. "No, thanks. I'll take your word for it. You were very brave. I am very grateful. Let's leave it at that."

Probably a good idea, Patrick thought, given the way she tempted him. Fortunately, before he could ignore his good sense, he heard voices and yet more footsteps on the dock. Apparently, no one in the whole blasted town could read, or else, like Alice, they were all starting to assume that the No Trespassing sign didn't apply to them.

Alice apparently heard the noise at the same time. "You obviously have company coming. I should go," she said a little too eagerly.

Given the choice between the company he knew and the uninvited guests outside, he opted for the familiar. "Stay," he commanded. "I'll get rid of whoever it is."

But when he stepped onto the deck, he saw not one or even two people who could be easily dismissed, but three, all dark-haired replicas of the man he'd come to hate—Connor Devaney.

"Patrick Devaney? Son of Kathleen and Connor?" one of them asked, stepping forward.

Patrick nodded reluctantly, his heart pounding. It couldn't be that these three men who looked so familiar were really his brothers. Not after all these years. And yet, somehow, he knew they were, as surely as if they'd already said the words.

"We're your brothers," the one in front said.

And with those simple yet monumental words, his past and present merged.

Chapter Four

A part of Patrick wanted to slam the door and pretend he'd never seen the men on the other side. He wanted to go on living the life he'd made for himself without family ties, without complications. These three men represented all sorts of uncomfortable complications.

Too late now, he thought, looking into eyes as blue as his own. He could already feel the connection pulling at him. It was an unbelievable sensation, knowing that three men he'd spent the past few years wondering about were now right here on his doorstep. He had yet to decide if that was good or bad, miracle or disaster. More than likely he wouldn't know for some time to come. The only way to tell would be to hear them out, see what sort of baggage they'd accumulated, thanks to being abandoned by their parents, and learn what their expectations were of him.

He scanned their faces with an eagerness that surprised him, looking for signs of resentment or blame. He saw only a certain wariness that was to be expected under the circumstances. These weren't old high school chums who'd come to call, but brothers—brothers he'd last seen when he was far too young for the concept to even register.

The one who'd spoken first seemed to sense his turmoil. "Did you know about us?" he asked, regarding Patrick worriedly. "Or did we just come busting in here and shock you into silence by telling you something you didn't know?"

"I knew about you," Patrick admitted reluctantly. When his words caused a flash of hurt to appear in one brother's eyes, Patrick quickly added, "But only for a few years now. Before that . . ." He shrugged. "I guess Daniel and I were just too young when we left to remember. I'm sorry. You have no idea how sorry."

"Don't be sorry. You were barely two when you left," his brother said. "How did you find out? Did our parents tell you?"

Patrick shook his head. "Daniel and I found some old photographs of us as babies. The three of you were in them. We asked our folks about the older boys in the pictures, and after a lot of denial, they finally admitted you were our brothers. We couldn't get them to say a lot more."

"Yeah, I imagine we're not their favorite topic," one of the others said with a bitterness that seemed to run as deep as Patrick's.

"Can it, Sean," the third one said, giving his brother's shoulder a squeeze. "Now's not the time. None of this is Patrick's fault."

"Given how we're related, it seems a little odd, but I guess introductions are in order," the first one said. "I'm Ryan, the oldest. I own an Irish pub in Boston."

Patrick would have guessed that, not just from

the few strands of gray in his black hair or the lines in his face, but because he was the obvious leader. He turned his gaze to the brother standing next to him, the one with broader shoulders and the quick tongue.

"And you?"

"I'm Sean, next to oldest, a Boston firefighter and the one who doesn't know enough to keep his opinions to himself." He gave Patrick a rueful half smile that didn't quite reach his eyes.

"Hey, I can relate to that," Patrick responded. "Whatever's in my head tends to come out of my mouth. Daniel, well, he's not like that. He was always the peacemaker."

Sean's half smile turned into a full-fledged grin. "Sort of like our Michael here," he said, poking the remaining brother in the ribs with his elbow. "He's such a pacifist, it's hard to believe he's an ex-SEAL."

Michael rolled his eyes, then stepped forward with a decided limp and held out his hand. "I'm Michael," he said quietly. "I'm just a couple of years older than you and Daniel."

"Oh, my, this is so incredible." The soft murmur came from behind Patrick.

He turned and stared into eyes shining with unshed tears. For a moment he'd forgotten all about Alice, but she'd apparently followed him up onto the deck when he hadn't immediately returned. Now he seized on her presence like a lifeline.

Needing desperately to hold on to something familiar, if only barely so, he reached for her hand. Alice held on tight, communicating surprising understanding and support. It was almost as if this reunion meant as much to her as it did to him. Once again Patrick wondered about her past and the sense he'd had that they had experienced similar losses in their lives—a loss of people, perhaps a loss of innocence.

"Can we go somewhere and talk?" Ryan asked. He glanced pointedly at Alice. "Or is this a bad time?"

"Absolutely not," Alice said.

She spoke quickly, as if sensing that Patrick might try to think of some way to put off this encounter until he'd regained his equilibrium. "Jess's is close. Why not go there?"

Since the unanimous opinion seemed to be that this conversation was going to take place, Patrick finally nodded. Jess's would be better and far less intimate than trying to crowd four big men into the tight quarters below deck on his boat, and the chill in the night air made sitting on deck an uncomfortable alternative, although it might have the effect of shortening the encounter.

Still, Ryan waited, watching him sympathetically. "Is this okay with you?" he asked Patrick. "I know we've barged in here without warning, but we've waited a long time for this moment. We weren't absolutely certain we had the right man, but one look at you and there was little question that you're our brother. We'd really like you to fill us in on some things."

Patrick fought off doubts and reminded himself that he'd always preferred to confront things head-on. "Sure, why not?" he said, as if the prospect of a beer and a little get-acquainted chitchat were of no consequence. Admittedly he had a great deal of curiosity about these men who were his brothers. He might as well satisfy it, now that the opportunity had presented itself.

Besides, there was something reassuringly solid and normal about the three older Devaneys. He'd learned a lot about judging people since leaving home. He could tell at first glance that these were men of character. One of them had been a SEAL, for heaven's sake. If that didn't speak of courage and honor, what did? Maybe it was possible to outfox the Devaney bad blood, after all. If so, he wanted to know how.

As he led the procession toward Jess's, his steps dragged. Even though he'd satisfied himself that this was the thing to do, he couldn't deny feeling a certain amount of dread. What if things were even worse for his brothers than he'd imagined? What if they bore scars from being left behind? What if they blamed him, right along with their parents? Not that it would be a rational blame, since he and Daniel had been little more than babies, but in a volatile situation, logic and reason seldom mattered. Though he didn't even know them, he found that he desperately wanted them to accept him, and that terrified him. Discovering his parents' betrayal had taught him never to expect or need too much from anyone. Better to be a loner than to be hurt like that ever again.

Besides, his brothers had said they were here to fill in the blanks in their lives, not to answer all of his thousand and one questions.

With Patrick lost in thought, Alice kept up a barrage of inconsequential, nonstop chatter, mostly about Widow's Cove's history. It helped to defuse the tension as they made their way to Jess's.

As they neared the bar, they could hear the jukebox blasting. That, too, could be an inadvertent blessing, Patrick concluded. It was going to make real conversation difficult, if not impossible. And at this time of the evening on a typical Friday, Jess's was usually packed and noisy. Maybe they wouldn't even find a free table, Patrick thought, in one last hopeful bid to put this encounter off until tomorrow . . . or maybe forever. Maybe Daniel had it right, after all. Maybe it was better to keep his head buried in the sand. Maybe these strangers who claimed to be his brothers would go away. Sure, his curiosity wouldn't be satisfied, but what did that matter really? He'd made it through more than twenty years without having them in his life, and vice versa.

His halfhearted hope for a quick end to the

evening was promptly dashed. He wasn't entirely sure how Alice managed it, but with a few whispered words to Molly, a table was magically cleared. Then Alice gave his hand one last reassuring squeeze. "I'll leave you with your brothers."

Fighting panic, Patrick gazed into her eyes. "Don't."

"You'll be fine," she assured him. "Obviously, I don't know the whole story, but I heard enough to know that this must be a life-altering moment for all of you. I don't belong here in the middle of it."

"I want you to stay," he said, needing some sort of familiar lifeline, someone from the world he'd made for himself to steady him as it rocked on its axis.

"It's okay," Ryan assured her. "If Patrick wants you here, it's fine with us."

Still, Alice shook her head and extracted her hand from the death grip Patrick had on it. "Thanks, but I need to get home. I'm glad I got to meet you, though."

Ryan nodded. "Perhaps we'll meet again one day," he said, then headed over to join the others.

Still, Patrick held back. "I never thanked you for the soup," he protested with ridiculous urgency, just to keep her there and talking.

She grinned at that, obviously seeing straight through him. "And now you have."

She pushed him none too gently toward the table

where his brothers were already seated. Patrick sighed and let her go, but his gaze followed her as she left the bar. Only then did he suck in a deep breath and go to join his brothers, pulling up a chair at the end of the booth rather than sliding into the vacant spot they'd left next to Michael.

"Pretty woman," Ryan observed. "Is she someone special?"

"I barely know her," Patrick said, forcing his attention to the three men seated opposite him like some sort of military tribunal. He should have slipped into the booth, he realized belatedly, made himself one of them, instead of an outsider. The symbolism was unmistakable. He wondered if they were aware of it.

Fascinated with the three men despite himself, he studied them. As Ryan had noted, there was no question about the family resemblance. All had the pitch-black hair and blue eyes of their Irish ancestors. He'd seen enough pictures of past generations—if not of this one—to know that Devaney men tended to be handsome rogues. Ryan's hair was a bit longer than the others and had those few errant strands of gray creeping in. He also had a tiny scar at the corner of his mouth.

Suddenly, completely out of the blue, a memory slammed into Patrick's head. There had been an argument, some sort of dispute between him and Daniel over a toy dump truck. Ryan had tried to mediate. Turning his temper on Ryan, Patrick had thrown the truck at him and split his lip. The image, obviously buried in his subconscious for years, was as clear now as if it had happened yesterday.

Tears swimming in his eyes, he swallowed hard and pointed at the scar. "I did that to you, didn't I? I threw a truck at you."

Surprise flickered in Ryan's eyes, then amusement. "I'll be damned. I'd forgotten that," he said, touching the scar as if he'd also forgotten its existence.

"You planning on getting even at this late date?" Patrick inquired warily.

Ryan rubbed his face. "Too late for that. I've been living with this face for a lot of years now. I'm used to it."

"Besides, Maggie thinks the scar's sexy," Sean chimed in with a grin.

"Maggie?" Patrick asked.

"His wife," Sean explained. "How he caught a wonderful woman like Maggie is beyond me, but I think that scar played a part in it."

Ryan laughed. "Could be. She does seem to be fond of kissing me, at any rate. I should probably thank you, Patrick, but I guess I'll let my wife do that when she meets you."

Patrick froze at the implication that they were here for more than some very brief get-acquainted meeting. This invasion of his turf was disturbing enough. He wasn't ready by a long shot for wives and maybe even kids.

He regarded his brothers warily. "What are you talking about?"

"I'm getting married," Michael explained. "That's why we picked this particular time to come looking for you."

"How long have you known where I was?"

Apparently, Ryan heard the tension in his voice. "Not that long. Honest. Besides, Michael was badly injured when Sean and I first found him. He wanted to be on his feet again before we came up here to see if we had the right man."

Patrick remembered the noticeable limp. "What happened?"

"A sniper attack," Michael said succinctly. "It ended my career as a SEAL. It's taken me a while to come to grips with that. In the meantime, I've been a bear to be around."

"That's an understatement. He was being a total pain in the butt till his physical therapist badgered him into getting out of his wheelchair just so he could catch her," Sean teased. "Talk about motivation. Kelly was damn good at it."

"Very funny," Michael retorted. "The bottom line is Kelly and I are getting married, and we'd all like you to come back to Boston next week for the wedding. That way we'll all have a chance to get to know each other. Daniel, too."

Patrick instinctively shook his head. As much as he'd thought about this moment, things were moving too fast for him. "I don't think so," he said, leaving aside the question of Daniel. The prospect of exchanging whatever tight-knit family ties they'd managed to forge for the ones he'd already broken held no appeal. Seeing them now was one thing. Exchanging an occasional Christmas card might be nice. But anything more was impossible.

Ryan regarded him with sympathy. "We're not a bad lot," he reassured Patrick. "And it's not as if we've been plotting and scheming together against you because you stayed with the folks and we didn't."

"I'm not worried about that," Patrick said. If only they knew how devastating it had been to learn that their parents weren't the models of decency that he'd always believed them to be.

"Really?" Sean asked skeptically. "I'm not sure the thought wouldn't have crossed my mind if I were in your position."

"That's because you're a cynic, Sean," Michael accused.

"Maybe he hates us for showing up here," Sean said, not backing down.

"I don't even know you," Patrick said. "As for hating you, why would I? You didn't do anything. If anything, you guys were the victims."

Ryan grinned. "What do you know? A Devaney with an open mind. Now that's something new."

"Oh, put a sock in it," Sean said good-naturedly.

Patrick listened to the bantering with amazement. "Can I ask you something?"

"Anything," Michael told him.

"After Mom and Dad took off with us, did you guys stick together? You seem so close, like the way Daniel and I used to be before . . . well, just before."

The three exchanged a significant look that spoke volumes. It was Ryan who responded. "No. We were separated and put into foster care."

Patrick got a sick feeling in the pit of his stomach. "With good families, at least?"

"My foster folks were the best," Michael said. "You'll meet them at the wedding. I've already filled them in about you. They can't wait to add another Devaney to the family. Hell, they've even opened their arms to these guys. Obviously, they're saints."

Ryan and Sean nodded. "That they are," Ryan said.

"Michael really lucked out in the foster family department," Sean said. "Mine were okay, but they were doing a job, you know what I mean?"

When Ryan remained silent, Patrick got the message. "You had a bad experience?"

"More like a dozen of them," Ryan said, though the words were expressed with surprisingly little evidence of bitterness. "But that got me to where I am now, so I have no reason to complain, I suppose. Not that I would have said that a few years ago. Meeting Maggie changed my outlook on a lot of things."

Patrick's anger at their parents deepened. "I'm sorry."

"Not your fault," Ryan said.

"Were you all in touch, at least?"

"Not until a few years ago for Ryan and Sean, and in my case, a few months ago," Michael told him. "Like I said, they tracked me down at a bad time in my life, right after my knee and thigh were shattered by that sniper and I was told I'd probably never walk again, much less go back to work as a SEAL."

"I'm amazed. You seem so well adjusted and so comfortable with each other," Patrick said. "I thought maybe . . . well, that you'd lucked out."

"Are you saying you didn't?" Ryan asked, his gaze sharpening. "What happened? Our folks didn't abuse you, did they?"

There was a protective note in his voice that stunned Patrick. "No," he said at once, not wanting them to get the wrong idea about his disenchantment with their parents. "Far from it. Daniel and I had it okay, actually. Mom and Dad did their best for us. Dad worked hard. I guess we were a typical family until Daniel and I found out about you guys. Then things kind of fell apart, at least for me. I couldn't believe what they'd done to you. They refused to offer one word of explanation or apology, so I took off and moved over here. I've seen Daniel once or twice in the past few years, but I haven't seen or spoken to Mom or Dad since I walked out. I don't think I'll ever be able to look them in the eyes again."

"You left because of us?" Sean said, sounding surprised.

Patrick nodded. "What they did, whatever reason they thought they had for doing it, it was wrong. It made me question everything I'd ever felt for them."

"That must have been hard," Michael said.

He was regarding Patrick with that sympathetic look that was beginning to get on his nerves. Why should his brothers feel sorry for him? They'd apparently gone through hell—or at least Ryan had—while Patrick had had a comparatively normal childhood. Evidently, though, they didn't want or expect his sympathy.

It was all too damn confusing. He suddenly wanted nothing more than to get back to his boat, to walk away from all of the conflicting emotions roiling around inside him. As for going to Boston for the wedding of a man he'd just met—or felt as if he had—forget it. It wasn't going to happen.

He stood up. "Look, I don't mean to be rude, but I honestly don't know why you came here. It can't be because you want another brother in your lives, especially one who got all the love and attention you should have gotten. And I sure as hell don't want to go to Boston and pretend that we're family."

"We *are* family," Ryan said quietly. "There's no

escaping that. And we didn't come here to mess up the life you've made for yourself. We just wanted you to know that we're out there and if you ever need us, all you have to do is shout."

They were being so nice, so reasonable, it made him want to scream. He didn't deserve the way they were reaching out to him.

"Look, the way I see it, we're not family, not in any way that counts," Patrick said.

"We've got the same blood flowing through our veins," Michael told him. "Devaney blood."

Patrick frowned at that. "To tell you the truth, I've just about had my fill of being a Devaney."

"Because of what our folks did to *us?*" Ryan asked. "We're the ones who got abandoned, not you. We're the ones who have a right to be angry, not you."

"No, Daniel and I were just lied to our whole lives," Patrick said bitterly. "Maybe that's not the same as what you went through, but trust me, it makes you question just about everything—and it sure as hell doesn't make you anxious to try the whole family thing on for size again."

He was out of the bar before any of them could think of a response. Then again, maybe none of them even cared enough to stop him. This visit had been all about satisfying some innate curiosity, but they'd done that now.

All the way back to the dock, Patrick worked to convince himself that he didn't give a damn whether they left the same way they'd come, without a word to let him know. He sank into a chair on the deck of his boat despite the chill in the air and sucked in a deep breath. If he'd expected the salt air and solitude to calm him, he was disappointed. He tried to focus on Alice, figuring a beautiful, tempting woman ought to be able to occupy his mind, but that failed him, too.

No matter what he tried, he couldn't make himself stop thinking about meeting his brothers after all these years. He told himself that little instant of nostalgia back at Jess's was just that, a momentary glimpse of a past so long ago it didn't matter. He'd meant what he said—he'd had his fill of being a Devaney. The only one he missed these days was Daniel, but he'd made his peace with that, too.

Given the turmoil of his thoughts and his inability to put his brothers out of his head, he wasn't totally stunned by the sound of footsteps approaching once again.

"Who's there?" he called out with a resigned sigh.

"Your brothers," a voice—Ryan's—responded emphatically. "You're not getting rid of us so easily, and we have three women back in Boston who will kill us if we don't talk you into coming back for the wedding."

"Knowing Ryan's Maggie, she'll come here and pester you till you give in," Michael agreed. "And Deanna and Kelly are no slouches in the persuasion department, either. You may as well cave in now and save yourself the humiliation of letting them get the better of you."

"Why would they care? Why would it matter to any of you whether I'm there or not?" he asked, completely bewildered that he mattered to people who were essentially strangers. His own parents and twin hadn't pestered him to stick around when he'd left home. He was pretty sure his parents had been half-relieved to see him go after he'd put them on the defensive about the past. They lived less than thirty miles away and had never bothered to seek him out. After Patrick's initial lack of welcome, Daniel had called a few times, but even he had given up eventually.

But these three strangers weren't giving up. How ironic was that? They stepped into the dim beam of light coming up from below deck. Once again it was Ryan who responded.

"We want you there because you're family," he said simply.

"A helluva family," Patrick noted.

"Yeah, well, we're all getting used to it," Sean said.

"We've all learned just how important family is," Michael added quietly.

"And some of us had further to go in that regard than others," Ryan added. "Believe me, if you'd run across me a few years back, you'd never have caught me touting the virtues of marriage and kids.

Now I have a wife I adore, a little girl who can wrap me around her finger and a baby on the way."

"Didn't the thought of all that terrify you?" Patrick asked curiously.

"You'd better believe it," Ryan admitted. "But once you meet Maggie, you'll see why I didn't stand a chance."

"I know you might feel a little awkward and out of place at first, but it won't last, believe me. Not with this crowd. Please, Patrick, won't you come?" Michael asked. "After that, if it's what you want, we'll leave you in peace, but at least you'll know where to find us if you ever change your mind and want us back in your life."

Patrick doubted it was possible they could leave him in peace. It had been a long time since he'd found any peace inside himself. And now he was more churned up than ever. He had a thousand and one questions he didn't want to have about these three brothers who'd popped into his life so unexpectedly.

He looked into three faces that were essentially mirror images of his own and nodded slowly. "What the hell? I've never been to Boston."

Michael grasped his hand and shook it, then abandoned the polite gesture and pulled him into a bear hug that pretty much knocked the breath out of him.

"I was as skeptical as you, when these two tracked me down in a hospital in San Diego,"

Michael told him, then grinned. "Turns out they're not so bad."

Patrick wasn't anywhere near ready to let go of his skepticism. "I think I'll reserve judgment," he said stiffly.

"You've got every right," Ryan said solemnly. "Mind if we ask you one more question?"

"I imagine you want to know about Daniel and our folks," Patrick said.

Sean nodded. "You said you took off, so that must mean they don't live here in Widow's Cove. Where are they?"

"Living about thirty miles from here last time I checked," he said with undisguised bitterness.

"When was that?" Michael asked.

"Six years ago," he said without emotion.

"And they haven't come after you?" Sean asked, then shook his head. "I don't know why the hell that should surprise me. They never looked for us." He exchanged a look with the others. "As long as we're this close, do you want to go over there?"

Ryan's gaze turned to Patrick. "We could include Daniel at least in the wedding, or would that make things uncomfortable for you?"

"It's up to Michael. It's his wedding," Patrick said grudgingly. He didn't even attempt to hide his distaste at the idea.

Michael searched his face, then nodded slowly in apparent understanding of the unspoken message.

"I think we can wait on contacting Daniel. At least we know where he is now."

Ryan seemed about to protest, then nodded. "Your call."

"I say we wait," Michael said.

Patrick couldn't hide his relief. "When the time comes, I'll give you a phone number and an address. I doubt it's changed since the last time I was in touch with them."

Ryan studied him intently. "If you feel like telling us about your life, we don't have anyplace we need to be till our flight back in the morning," he said quietly.

Patrick suspected it wasn't so much his life they cared about, but the family that had excluded them. He wasn't up to it. It had been a day full of shocks, too many to end it by reliving one of the worst periods in his life.

He looked his oldest brother in the eye and promised, "Another time, okay?"

"That's fine, then," Ryan said agreeably. "We'll get on back to our motel. You going fishing in the morning, or can you join us for breakfast?"

Patrick longed to say he was going fishing. It would be the truth. That was usually how he spent his Saturdays. But something compelled him to make the time for these three men who'd searched for him. Whatever their reasons were, however little he wanted to care about them, they were his brothers. He knew what that sort of relationship could mean. He and Daniel had been close once, able to talk about anything, able to count on each other. He'd lost that, and he found the possibility that he could have that sort of tightknit relationship again more alluring than he'd ever imagined possible.

"I'll be at Jess's at eight," he said. "If you're interested, Molly makes a pretty decent omelette."

"The omelette sounds good," Ryan said. "But the conversation sounds even better. We'll see you then, little brother."

Patrick watched the three of them walk off into the darkness with a sense of wonder. They looked as if they'd always been together, always been a team. And suddenly he felt more alone than he'd ever felt before.

Chapter Five

With the tables filled with locals and tourists, Molly was moving at her usual brisk pace when Patrick wandered into Jess's. Her step faltered at the unusual sight of him at this hour on a Saturday morning, then she plastered a smile on her face.

"It must have been some night. You look like hell," she said cheerfully. "Go on over to the bar and I'll pour you a cup of strong coffee in a minute."

"I'll need a table," Patrick responded. "Four cups of coffee."

She nodded, clearly not half as startled by the request as he'd anticipated. "Over there, then." She gestured toward a more private booth in the back. "I'll be right there with the coffee."

His brothers still hadn't arrived by the time Molly brought the coffee, which meant she had no reason at all not to slip into the booth opposite him and study him with that frank, assessing look that meant she was about to start poking around in his life.

"Don't start with me, Molly," he said, hoping to forestall the inquisition.

"Is it a crime to want to know what's going on in the life of a man I consider to be a friend? Alice told me that those were your brothers who turned up here last night. I think I have a right to be curious," she said. Regarding him sympathetically, she asked, "Does Daniel know they've turned up?"

"I'm surprised you care what Daniel knows," he said.

"I don't," she insisted. "I'm merely curious."

"Okay, then, if it's only to satisfy your *curiosity,* he doesn't know," Patrick said tightly. "At least not from me. Who knows what someone in here last night might have felt the need to pass along to him."

She frowned at his testy tone. "Are you okay, Patrick? If you need to talk about this, you know I'll listen."

He shrugged off the question and the offer. "Why wouldn't I be okay?"

She frowned at him. "Is that all I'm going to get out of you on the subject?"

"Yep."

"Okay, fine," she said, giving up a little too readily. "Let's talk about you and Alice, instead."

Patrick glowered at her, but she knew him too well to be intimidated. It was one of his greatest frustrations that he'd lost the power to keep some people at a distance. Molly was the first to breach his reserve. Now Alice was gathering insights like little nuggets she could assemble to figure him out.

"I suppose you think that's off-limits, too," Molly said, when he remained stubbornly silent.

"It is," he said tightly. "Mainly because there *is* no me and Alice to discuss."

Molly rolled her eyes, clearly not buying it. "If you say so."

"I do," he said quite firmly. "And here come my brothers now, so make yourself scarce. Don't start poking and prodding at them."

"I imagine you won't object if I at least take your breakfast order?" she said tartly.

He grinned. "There you go, Molly. You could get the hang of being the polite hostess of this place yet."

"Don't count on it where you're concerned," she retorted, sliding out of the booth, then turning a beaming smile on his brothers. "Hi. I'm Molly. Your coffee's in the pot on the table, and I'll be back to take your order in a few minutes. As for him," she said, nodding toward Patrick, "try teaching him some manners."

"Too late for that, I imagine," Ryan said, grinning back at her. "And I doubt he'd take advice from us, anyway."

"You could at least try," she said.

"What did you do to rile the lovely waitress?" Sean inquired, studying Patrick.

"The lovely waitress is the owner of this place, and she takes after her grandfather Jess," Patrick said. "She thinks there's nothing that goes on in here or in all of Widow's Cove that's not her business."

"In other words, she was asking about us," Michael guessed.

Patrick nodded. "And when I refused to satisfy

her curiosity on that count, she moved on to Alice."

"Which brings up a point," Michael said. "It never occurred to me to ask last night, but would you like to bring her to the wedding?"

Patrick held up both hands. "Whoa! I barely know the woman. I don't think a wedding is the best idea for a first date."

"You've never even been out on a date with her?" Ryan asked, clearly shocked. "The two of you seemed pretty tight last night. You were awfully reluctant to let her leave."

"We met earlier in the day," Patrick explained, then told the story of Ricky Foster's untimely nosedive off his pier.

"Interesting," Sean said. "Our brother seems to be following our pattern of meeting his soul mate under unusual circumstances. Ryan's Maggie wandered into his pub after having a flat tire on Thanksgiving eve. I met Deanna after I put out the fire that destroyed her apartment. And Kelly came into Michael's life after he was shot."

"Alice is not my soul mate," Patrick protested, ignoring the fact that he had been more drawn to her than he had been to any other woman in a long time. That was chemistry, not some mystical connection. And whatever it was, he intended to ignore it, for sure.

"Denial," Michael noted, grinning. "Another part of the pattern."

"Yep, he's got it bad," Ryan teased.

Patrick gave the three of them a sour look. "Gee, if I'd known having big brothers was this much fun, I'd have gone hunting for you years ago."

Molly arrived just then, looking particularly pleased to find them all laughing. "I'm delighted you all turned up when you did," she said.

Ryan looked up at her. "Oh?"

"Patrick was getting a little too hermity, if you know what I mean."

"Molly," Patrick warned, his voice low.

She gave him an innocent look. "Is something wrong?"

"You're treading on thin ice," he said.

"Is that so?" She stomped her foot on the old oak floor. "Seems solid enough to me." She turned to Ryan. "You seem like a man who knows his own mind. What can I get you?"

After she'd taken all their orders and gone, Ryan turned to Patrick. "Just how many women do you have in your life, little brother?"

"None," he said flatly.

All three brothers hooted at that.

"Look, did you come here this morning just to pester me about my love life? If so, I can leave now and still get in a few hours of fishing."

"I guess we're crossing the line," Sean said, though his eyes were twinkling with amusement.

"Definitely," Michael agreed.

"But this is such a fascinating topic, I hate to pass on it," Sean added.

"Maybe that's because we'd rather hear about the women in Patrick's life than talk about our folks," Ryan said wryly.

Sean and Michael instantly sobered, all teasing gone from their expressions.

"You've got that right," Sean said bitterly.

"Since I'm not crazy about talking about them, either, let's not," Patrick said. "We could talk about baseball. How do you guys think the Red Sox are going to do this year?"

Sean seemed eager to go along with the change of topic, but Ryan promptly cut him off.

"Locking the past in a closet doesn't work," Ryan countered. "Lord knows I tried for a lot of years. Now that I'm close to getting everything out in the open, I want to finish up so I can forget about it once and for all."

"There's just one problem with that," Patrick said. "I don't have the answers you want. Like I told you last night, the folks refused to answer any of the questions Daniel and I threw at them. As far as I know, they haven't opened up with him since I walked out. I think he'd have let me know if they had. If you want answers, you're going to have to look them up yourselves. I'll tell you where to find them, but that's it. Depending on what time your flight is, you could go today. It's only about a thirty-minute drive."

All three of his brothers fell silent at the suggestion. It was as if having finally neared the end of their long search, they weren't particularly anxious to start that final leg.

Ryan sighed heavily, his gaze on Michael. "Up to you. Do you want this over and done with before the wedding? Or will it ruin what should be the happiest time of your life?"

"I won't let our folks ruin anything for me," Michael said flatly. "But I still think we should wait. Finding them is going to affect all of us, and frankly I want all your attention focused on the wedding. If I walk into that church without the rings or miss the rehearsal dinner because you guys had your minds on what happened up here in Maine, Kelly will never let any of us forget it."

"You sure you don't want to make peace so the folks can be at the wedding?" Ryan persisted.

"*My* family will be at the wedding," Michael said emphatically. "The Havilceks and you guys are the only family I need to have there."

Ryan nodded. "Then we'll drop it for now," he told Patrick.

Patrick couldn't help the sigh of relief that shuddered through him.

"Since we've put the topic of the folks on the back burner for now," Sean said, a mischievous twinkle in his eyes again, "then I suggest we talk some more about Alice and Patrick. We owe it to our baby brother to see that he's on the path toward marital bliss like the rest of us. We can't have him up here living like a hermit, the way Molly says he is."

"Molly has a big mouth," Patrick complained, just as she arrived with the food.

"Watch it, buster," she said, "or you could wind up wearing these eggs."

"Just speaking the truth," he said unrepentantly.

"It's never wise to accuse your friendly neighborhood bartender of having a big mouth," Molly warned. "She might be tempted to spill all your secrets to certain interested parties."

"I don't have any secrets," Patrick retorted.

"I don't know. I think your brothers might be interested in knowing how lonely you've been since you left home. And while I never could figure out how you wound up with a brother as uptight and impossible as Daniel, I know you miss having him around."

He noticed his brothers watching him with a speculative look in their eyes and mentally cursed Molly for opening up that particular can of worms.

Patrick scowled at her. "There went your tip," he said, trying to inject a light note into his voice.

She shrugged. "Something tells me the rest of this crew will make up for it."

With that she strolled off to wait on other customers, who, Patrick surmised, probably managed to have their breakfasts served without the added ingredient of Molly's sass.

"Want to talk about it?" Ryan asked. "Is Molly right?"

"If you're asking if I miss Daniel, he's my twin—what the hell do you think?" he said heatedly. "Of course I miss him! But I'm not interested in mending that particular fence. He chose to stick by our parents." He looked his brothers in the eyes. "So you see, I know a little something about being shut out of the Devaney clan, too. And just because I was eighteen when I walked away doesn't mean it was a helluva lot easier on me than it was on you. I'd planned on college, but leaving home shot the hell out of that. I had to work. Fortunately, I love what I do. Being out on the water can be a hard life, but it's a good one."

Michael gave him a knowing look. "Amen to that. Not a day goes by that I don't miss being a SEAL. I almost took up a career as captain of a charter fishing boat, but the Navy convinced me that had a better use for my talents, even if it did stick me behind a desk. Still, I never miss a chance to get out on the water."

"You'll have to come up here sometime and go out with me," Patrick said, enjoying the sense of camaraderie he felt with his brother. Daniel had never loved the sea as much as Patrick did, and he certainly didn't understand Patrick's decision to become a fisherman rather than taking one dime of his college money from their parents.

Michael grinned at the invitation. "I'd like that.

As for family, you have us now," he said. "We aren't your twin, but we are your brothers and we stick together."

Ryan nodded. "I went looking for these guys because I wanted to put the past to rest once and for all. I never expected to find men I felt connected to from the instant I laid eyes on them."

"Same with me," Sean said.

Michael nodded. "And me."

"And I feel the same about you," Ryan said to Patrick. "We've always been your brothers by blood, but from this moment on we'll be your family in every sense of the word, if you'll let us."

Patrick thought he'd long since passed the stage of being sentimental about family, but he found himself fighting against the unexpected sting of tears. He'd had no idea just how much he'd missed having family in his life until the prospect of having it again was dangled in front of him. Could he make himself reach out for it? Could he risk another hurt, another betrayal?

He honestly didn't know. And he had no idea at all how long it would take him to figure it out.

Alice usually spent Saturday mornings cleaning the little cottage she'd fixed up when she'd returned to Widow's Cove. She'd used the money she'd inherited from her parents to turn their home into her own. She'd once vowed never to set foot in it again and she hadn't, not until after they were gone. She had held on to all the anger right up until the second the policeman on the phone had told her about the accident. Then, in a heartbeat, she couldn't seem to recall why they had fought or why she had let it matter for so many years. Clinging to hurt had been cold comfort while she'd been all alone in Boston.

She sighed at the memory and tried to motivate herself to get busy with her chores. It didn't take all that long to run a vacuum through the four tiny rooms or to dust the few antiques she'd acquired since moving back. Still, it gave structure to her weekend, the two free days that always stretched out endlessly with way too many hours to think about the past.

She could hardly wait for warm weather to settle in for good so she could work in the garden she'd planned. She wanted spiky pink hollyhocks and bright day lilies to line the white picket fence of the seaside cottage. On the tiny patch of land in back she planned an herb garden. Her newly renovated home in Widow's Cove was going to be nothing at all like the dreary home in which she'd grown up. Her mother's taste had run to heavy drapes, plain white walls and sparse landscaping. Alice's walls were a cheery yellow, the woodwork white and white sheers billowed at her windows and let in lots of light and incredible shades of blue in the views of sky and sea.

Normally a thorough housecleaning, followed

by an afternoon poring through gardening books, would have occupied her on a day like this, but today she was far too restless to sit still or even to clean. All she could think about was the amazing scene on Patrick's boat the night before, when his three brothers had shown up out of the blue.

As she'd followed him up to the deck and listened to their exchange, she'd been stunned, but Patrick's shock had been almost palpable. The fact that he'd turned to her and all but pleaded for her to stay had touched her more than she wanted to admit. It had been a long time since anyone other than her students had needed her for anything. There was something about a usually strong man turning vulnerable that could twist her inside out, too. She'd fallen just a little bit in love with Patrick Devaney at that moment.

As soon as she finished tidying up in the kitchen after her breakfast, she automatically reached into the closet for her cleaning supplies, only to put them right back. The curiosity was killing her. She had to know how last night had turned out. Patrick had been given the chance she'd always dreamed about, a chance at a reconciliation with his family. Had he taken advantage of it?

She wasn't quite brave enough to risk another visit to Patrick's boat, but there was someone who'd have the answers she was after. Because yesterday's balmy breezes were a thing of the past, and a cold front had turned the air wintry once more, she pulled on her sheepskin-lined jacket and headed for Jess's.

"I was wondering when you'd turn up," Molly called out cheerfully when Alice stepped inside the dimly lit room. The window facing the street let in precious little light even on a sunny morning like this one.

"I'm not *that* predictable," Alice replied with a hint of indignation as she approached the bar.

"You are to someone who's known you since grade school," Molly said, then chided, "even if I don't see nearly enough of you these days."

Alice slid onto a stool and faced her friend. "I'm sorry."

"Don't apologize, just start coming around a bit more. You class up the place."

Alice laughed. "Hardly. If anything, having the kindergarten teacher around will kill your business."

"Since your visiting is such a rare thing, to what do I owe the honor . . . or need I ask? I imagine you came by to find out what went on with Patrick after you left last night," Molly said, giving her a sly once-over.

"Why would you think that?" Alice asked, as heat crept into her cheeks.

"Oh, please! When you were in here with the kids yesterday, you were watching the man as if he were covered in Belgian chocolate and you were in desperate need of a major fix of the stuff. You were no better last night."

"Don't be ridiculous!" Alice protested indignantly.

Molly grinned. "Then I suppose it is of absolutely no interest to you that he's sitting over in the corner, brooding over his fourth cup of coffee."

Alice barely resisted the sudden desire to bury her burning face in her hands. "He's here?"

"Has been for a couple of hours now. His brothers just left."

"Why didn't you say something sooner?" Snippets of their conversation came back to her. "Molly, what if he heard?"

"Honey, he's lost in his own thoughts. And I wasn't exactly shouting, you know. I do know a little bit about being discreet."

"Since when?" Alice asked, getting in her own barb. "Aren't you the girl who kept a record of the boys she'd kissed on the front of her English notebook in seventh grade?"

"I'm better now," Molly said primly. "All the juicy stuff about my love life is in the journal beside my bed." She studied Alice intently. "So, are you going to go over there or not?"

Alice glanced across the room and spotted Patrick in the corner. He was staring into his mug of coffee as if he'd never before seen anything so fascinating . . . or so sad.

Alice made a decision on impulse, something she'd done more in the past two days than she had in years. "Pour me two cups of coffee," she told Molly.

"Want me to slip a little Irish whiskey in his? It might loosen his tongue. I tried earlier, but I couldn't get a word out of him."

Alice was tempted, but she shook her head. If she could get a shy five-year-old to start chattering like a magpie, surely she could deal with one stoically silent male.

Coffee in hand, she crossed the room and slid into the booth opposite Patrick. He didn't even seem to notice her until she shoved one mug under his nose. Then he blinked and stared.

"Where'd you come from?" he asked, sounding cranky and not the least bit delighted to see her.

Relieved at the evidence that he'd heard none of Molly's teasing, she ignored the lack of welcome. "Are you asking in the cosmic sense?"

A half smile tugged at his lips. "It's too early in the morning for that."

"It's past ten."

Clearly startled, he stared at the clock over the bar. "How the hell did that happen?"

"The usual way. Time goes by, tick-tock, minute by minute."

"Very funny." He sat back and studied her, the tension in his shoulders visibly easing. "So, Alice Newberry, what are you doing hanging out in a bar at ten o'clock on a Saturday morning? Do the parents of your students know where you spend your free time?"

She bit back the first response that popped into her head. It would be way too revealing to admit that this was the first Saturday morning she'd ever ventured into Jess's. Patrick might have been lost in thought there for a minute, but he wasn't dense. He'd likely make the connection between her presence here today and his the night before. She didn't want him guessing that she was here to check on the outcome of his meeting with his brothers, after she'd made such a point of not intruding on it.

"Actually, I move from bar to bar so they can't keep up with me," she retorted. "This is my week for Jess's."

"How convenient for me," he said with what sounded like complete sincerity. "Have you eaten?"

"Hours ago," she admitted, almost regretting her early-morning habit of fixing a hearty breakfast to get her through a day that too often had no more than a few stolen minutes to grab a bite of lunch.

"Had enough coffee?"

"As a matter of fact, yes."

"Feel like going out on the boat for a couple of hours?"

"Sure," she said at once, telling herself it was

only because he seemed eager for the company. "But for the record, I don't know anything about fishing."

"I know enough for both of us," he said, tossing some money on the table and grabbing his jacket. He shrugged into it, then held hers so she could slip it on.

He gazed into her eyes as he pulled her jacket snugly around her. "Besides, I just feel like getting out on the water. The salt air clears my head. The fish'll be there come Monday morning."

"If you want to clear your head, are you sure you want me along?" Alice asked.

"I wouldn't have asked you if I didn't want you there," he said. "Ask Molly," he added, raising his voice and nodding toward the woman who was blatantly eavesdropping. "I rarely do anything I don't want to do."

"That's true enough," Molly confirmed. "Have fun, you two. And you can both thank me later."

Patrick stared blankly at Alice. "Thank her for what?"

Alice knew but wished she didn't. "Believe me," she said fervently, "you don't want to know."

Chapter Six

Patrick wasn't used to having anyone on board when he took the boat out, but Alice made a good companion. She didn't pester him with a lot of questions. In fact, she seemed perfectly content to sit on deck with a blanket wrapped around her and her face tilted up to the sun's rays. The wind was whipping her hair, but once again she seemed oblivious to the tangle.

"Your nose is getting sunburned," he said, tapping her gently on the tip of it before dropping down into the chair beside her.

She blinked in surprise, then yawned. "I think I dozed off."

"Must be my scintillating company," he said wryly.

She glanced around. "Not that I'm nervous or anything, but if you're sitting over here, who's piloting the boat?"

"I dropped anchor a few minutes ago," he explained.

"Where are we?"

"Not that far offshore, actually, just far enough away to keep from being bothered."

She grinned. "I gather you've concluded that the No Trespassing sign has lost its effectiveness."

He chuckled. "Given the parade coming down the dock yesterday, pretty much. From now on, if I want total peace and quiet, I'm moving out to sea."

"How come you invited me along, if you want total peace and quiet?"

"Maybe I knew you'd fall asleep the second you got a good dose of sea air," he teased, and pulled a tube of suntan lotion from his shirt pocket. He put a dab of the cream on his finger and spread it across her nose, then onto her cheeks. Her skin was so soft he lingered, reluctant to stop touching her. His gaze drifted to hers and lingered there, as well. The sudden and totally unexpected spark of desire in her eyes stunned him and sent a jolt of sexual tension racing straight through him.

Before he could think it through, he was following his instincts, leaning forward, his mouth covering hers. She uttered a faint gasp of surprise, then moved into the kiss with an eagerness that once again caught him off guard. The kiss turned greedy and hot in a flash that almost brought him to his knees. Who would have thought that the sweet little kindergarten teacher packed a wallop like that? He was shaky when he finally had the sense to pull back.

"Don't stop," she whispered, sending yet another jolt through him. She reached out and touched his cheek. "Please. It's been forever since anyone kissed me like that. It felt good, No, it felt great."

Her honesty rattled him. "Alice . . ." The protest formed in his head but died when she took the matter out of his hands by leaning forward and kissing him, holding on as if he had something to offer that she'd been missing for eons.

Who knew where it would have led had it not been for the blast of a ship's horn that shattered the silence. Alice was trembling, the color in her cheeks high, when he reluctantly pulled away for the second time.

"We aren't by any chance bobbing around out here right in the path of some cruise ship, are we?" she asked without any real evidence of fear.

"Nope. That was just a friendly greeting," he assured her.

"And a timely one," she said with obvious regret. "I don't know what I was thinking. I'm not in the habit of attacking men I barely know."

"I kissed you first," he reminded her, then added solemnly, "Besides, kissing isn't about thinking. It's about feeling." He tilted her chin up and met her gaze. There was no mistaking her need for reassurance, so he gave it to her. "I haven't felt like that in a long time, Alice."

She swallowed hard, her gaze drifting away, then back as she finally admitted, "Me, neither."

"Why is that?" he asked, wondering whether someone had broken her heart.

"Bad choices and the sudden realization that I needed to figure out why I was making them."

"Did you reach any conclusions?"

"A few."

"Care to share them?"

"And ruin your image of me? I don't think so."

"You don't know what my image of you is," he pointed out.

"You think I'm a little ditzy, a lot naive and very prim," she said.

Patrick chuckled. "That was my first impression. It's been changing quickly."

"I probably shouldn't ask about your current impression."

"Probably not," he agreed.

He looked into her eyes and instantly the laughter died on his lips. From the moment they'd met, Patrick had had the feeling that he was no longer in control, that something bigger had taken over. He'd blamed it on the circumstances of their meeting, on his brothers, on anything other than the attraction that was so obviously simmering now.

"So, what are we going to do about all of this, Alice Newberry?" he asked.

"Nothing, if we're smart."

Patrick grinned at that. "Then isn't it wonderful that no one's ever accused me of doing the smart thing? How about you?"

"I *always* do the smart thing."

Somehow he doubted that. He had the sense that she'd only recently made a resolution to do the right thing, but that she wasn't quite living up to it yet. He rubbed his thumb across her lips, saw the flash of excitement stir in her eyes once more.

"Then I suppose one of us will have to change," he said.

Her mouth curved into a faint hint of a smile. "I suppose so."

He glanced sideways and gave her a lazy once-over. "You any good at change?"

"Not much."

"Neither am I." He reached for her hand and laced their fingers together. "How about this for now? There's nothing too dangerous about holding hands, is there?"

"Nothing at all," she agreed, leaning back in the chair and closing her eyes against the sun's glare, and quite possibly against his probing looks.

Patrick felt himself drifting off, oddly comforted by the feel of her soft, delicate hand in his much larger, rough one. What was it about a woman's touch that had the power to soothe when nothing else worked, he wondered.

The highly emotional meeting with his brothers faded from his mind. The complications ahead didn't seem to matter. All that mattered at this instant was the warmth of the sun on his face, the gentle rocking of the boat and the woman beside him. Life didn't get much better than this . . . unless, of course, a little hot, steamy sex was added in.

He fought a grin and resisted the desire to sneak a glance at Alice. Best not to go there. That one stolen kiss of his had unleashed unexpected passion in her. While he'd never been averse to uncomplicated, energetic sex, he had a feeling slipping into bed with Alice was going to be anything but uncomplicated. Besides, he'd hate to prove his brothers right about his level of involvement with Alice only a few brief hours after heatedly denying that he had any feelings for the woman.

Yes, indeed, he thought, his eyes clamped tightly shut, definitely best not to go there.

Alice could feel Patrick's gaze on her, but she absolutely, flatly refused to open her eyes. She was still simmering with embarrassment over her too-eager response to his kiss. What must he think of her? She'd all but crawled into his lap the instant he'd locked lips with her. She'd turned what might have been meant as an innocent, exploratory kiss into something wild and dangerous. She'd been so startled by her uncharacteristic reaction, it was a wonder she hadn't jumped overboard just to cool herself off.

Finally, when she felt his grip on her hand ease, she slipped her hand out of his and sighed. Risking a glance, she saw that he'd fallen asleep. His impressive chest was rising and falling with each steady breath he took. His long, dark eyelashes rested against his deeply tanned skin like smudges of coal. His lips—his magnificent, sweetly provocative lips—were curved into a half smile, as if he were dreaming something wonderful. She could have looked at him all day . . . and all night. The thought made her shiver with a sense of anticipation.

It would happen, too. She could feel it. The attraction wasn't one-sided. What she'd told Patrick was true. It had been so long since she'd felt anything like it.

When she'd first left home, she'd been so overwhelmed with work and difficult college classes that she'd had little time for romance. In her senior year, with the end of school in sight, she'd finally allowed herself the freedom to date and promptly fallen for the first man who'd asked her out.

Greg had turned out to be more interested in sharing her apartment than her life. She'd caught him at home, in their bed, with another classmate. An hour later everything he owned was on the lawn outside and he was sputtering protests and explanations even as she slammed the door in his face. It had taught her a lesson about getting involved too quickly.

Or at least she thought it had until she fell for the next man she went out with almost as rapidly. That hadn't ended quite as badly or as painfully, but it had been doomed from the outset. She would have seen that if she'd given the relationship a hard look at the beginning.

She'd spent the next couple of years taking a good long look at herself and her tendency to fall in love at the drop of a hat. It hadn't taken a genius to figure out that she was trying to find a replacement for the family she'd turned her back on. As the song said, she'd been looking for love in all the wrong places.

Until yesterday she'd thought she'd broken the pattern, but now here she was, all-too-fascinated with Patrick, and they hadn't so much as had a first date yet. Well, she wasn't going to make the same old mistake, no matter how tempting it might be. She was going to be smart this time, even if kissing him gave her a momentary sense of being connected and filled a huge void in her life.

Besides, there were flashing neon warning signs practically posted all around the man. He was a self-professed loner. He had major issues with his family. He was drifting through his life, quite literally at the moment, she thought wryly. He was the last man on earth she had any business falling for. She didn't even have to take one of those long, hard looks at the situation to figure that much out. Not that her hormones seemed to give two figs about any of that. Her body seemed to care only that he was a top-of-the-line kisser.

"Everything okay?" he asked, his voice husky with sleep.

"Sure," she said, a little too brightly. "Why?"

"You were frowning."

"Just wrestling with some old demons," she said, keeping her voice light.

"Who won?"

107

"I suppose that remains to be seen," she said honestly.

"Tell me about yourself," he encouraged, regarding her with unmistakable interest.

"There's not much to tell."

"You're from Widow's Cove, though, right?"

She nodded.

"Why don't I remember you from school? I thought I knew all the beautiful girls."

She grinned at the puzzlement in his voice. "I'm sure you did," she said. "I wasn't beautiful, and I was two years older, but I certainly knew who you were."

"Is that so?" he said with a hint of all-male arrogance.

She ticked off the obvious reason why the awareness had been so one-sided. "Star football player even as a sophomore. Advance placement in most of your classes. Girls falling at your feet. You were already a legend."

"And you let that scare you off?" he taunted.

"Absolutely. Besides, senior girls did not give sophomore boys a second look," she said airily, as if that had had anything at all to do with it. "We didn't want anyone thinking we were so desperate we had to rob the cradle."

"Oh, I think I could have held my own with you."

"No question about it," Alice said. "But senior girls had a reputation to maintain, even the quiet ones like me."

"So, who did you date?"

"No one. I just had one goal back then, to get away. I wasn't about to let romance interfere. I headed for Boston the day after graduation."

His gaze narrowed. "And never came back?"

"Not until last summer."

"What happened last summer to finally get you back home?"

"My parents were killed in a car accident," she said, surprised that she could actually say the words without getting choked up.

His expression immediately sobered. "I'm sorry. That must have been rough."

"You have no idea. We'd never reconciled. I will regret that till the day I die." She gave him a sideways look. "Let that be a lesson to you. We never know how long we're going to have to mend fences with the people we love."

"Some fences can't be mended," Patrick said.

"They must be," she insisted.

"Alice, I can see where you're coming from, but trust me, in my case, you don't know what the hell you're talking about. If you understood the whole story—"

"Tell me," she urged.

He shook his head. "There's no point. The past is what it is."

"And your brothers, where do they fit in?"

"That remains to be seen."

"Will you be seeing them again?"

"I agreed to go to Boston in a few days for Michael's wedding. After that, who knows?" he said with a shrug, as if it didn't matter to him one way or the other.

Alice ignored the shrug and went with what she thought she saw in his eyes, a need so raw that it probably scared him to death. She could relate to that only too well.

"Don't leave it to chance," she told him. "Do whatever it takes to keep them in your life."

His jaw tensed. "Again, not your call to make."

"I know that," she said impatiently. "But I also know what it's like to live with regrets, to know that it's too late to fix things. I wouldn't wish that on anyone. I don't want that for you."

"Why do you give a damn about any of this?" he asked. "You hardly know me."

"I know you better than you think," she said. "For a lot of years, I *was* you. I was angry and resentful and completely closed off from my parents. I made them miserable, and I lost something important that I can never get back. It's not too late for you to avoid the mistakes I made."

Patrick's expression softened ever so slightly. "I see where you're coming from, I really do, but I have to handle this my way, Alice. Maybe it's better if we steer clear of this particular topic from here on out."

She shook her head. "We can't, not if we're going to be friends. It'll be like the elephant in the room that we're trying to pretend isn't there. We can disagree over what to do about it, but we can't ignore it, Patrick."

"Friends, huh? That's how you see us, even after that steamy kiss?"

"Absolutely."

"That kiss didn't feel anything at all like a friendly peck," he noted.

Alice chuckled despite herself. "Which is why we're turning over a new leaf here and now. No more kisses."

Patrick groaned.

"I take it you disagree."

"I think that's pretty much as futile as trying to prevent a swamped boat from sinking by bailing with a teacup. It's not going to happen."

"I can control my urges, can't you?"

He reached for her hand and turned it over in his palm. She felt the warmth, the sandpapery, callused texture of a hand that worked hard. He rubbed his thumb across her wrist and sent heat spiraling through her to settle low in her belly. Her pulse jumped and he grinned.

"Still think you've got total control over those urges?" he asked.

"Maybe not total control," she admitted. "I'm working on it."

"Why fight the inevitable?"

"We are not inevitable," she insisted, even as she admitted to herself that she was lying through her teeth. Old patterns died hard. A part of her was falling fast, but she knew exactly how little judgment that part of her tended to exercise. She intended to fight it with every ounce of common sense she possessed. Real love didn't happen after two or three passing encounters. And she wasn't the kind of woman who could have a casual fling just because a man appealed to her.

She drew in a deep breath and steadied her racing pulse. Not this time. This time she was going to be smart and in control of her hormones and her emotions. Besides, if Patrick was destined to ignore the wisdom she'd gained from her own mistakes, she didn't want to be around for the train wreck that followed. And that wreck really was inevitable. She could already see it coming.

It had been a perfectly pleasant, lazy afternoon, right up until the moment when Alice had gotten that bee in her bonnet about his family. Patrick regretted more than he could say that she knew anything at all about his history with his folks or his recent reunion with his older brothers. He had a hunch she could be a worse nag than Molly, and that was saying something.

Still, he wasn't totally inclined to send her packing the instant they returned to the dock. He enjoyed provoking her, seeing the quick rise of heat in her cheeks, the flash of desire in her eyes that she was trying so hard to ignore.

"Want to stay for dinner?" he asked. "I could run over to Jess's and bring back some of Molly's chowder, and there's half a loaf of your bread left."

She turned those golden eyes of hers on him with a sorrowful expression. "What would be the point?"

"Staving off starvation," he suggested wryly.

She frowned at that. "You know that's not what I meant. Sooner or later, we'll just butt heads again."

"I've got a hard head. I can take it," Patrick assured her.

She fought a grin. "Isn't that the problem, your hard head?"

"Only if you let it be," he responded. "We could play cards after dinner. Where's the harm in that?"

Her gaze narrowed speculatively. "Poker?"

"If that's what you want to play," he agreed, hiding his surprise at the choice. He'd figured on a few hands of gin rummy, maybe.

"Okay, you're on," she said. "But I'll warn you here and now that I'm very, very good."

Something in her voice alerted him that she was dead serious.

"Where'd you learn to play?" he asked, suddenly cautious.

"In Jess's back room."

Patrick stared at her. "Jess taught you to play poker?"

"When Molly and I were about ten."

"I see."

She grinned. "Still want to take me on?"

"More than ever," he said with heartfelt enthusiasm that wasn't entirely based on her self-proclaimed poker-playing ability.

"Then get the chowder," she said. "I need stamina."

"Is the chowder going to do it?"

"If Molly made an apple pie today, a slice of that would help, too." Her expression turned thoughtful. "And maybe some chocolate. Molly keeps a stash of Hershey bars behind the counter. Two ought to do it."

Patrick chuckled. Everyone in town knew about Molly's cache of chocolate. When she ran out, it was best to steer clear until she'd replenished her supply. Toughened seamen tended to slip extra candy bars into the box just to assure a pleasant Molly who wouldn't take offense at some slip of the tongue and dump a beer over their heads.

"Should I risk asking or just steal the candy?" Patrick inquired.

"Ask," she said. "And do it politely. It's too late to get any chocolate from the drugstore. It closes at five."

"Aye, aye," Patrick said. "Shall I grab a couple of beers, too?"

She shuddered. "With chocolate? Are you crazy?"

Patrick grinned. "Coffee, then. There's some below deck. You can make it while I'm gone."

"Well, hell," she muttered with a pretty little pout. "I was counting on that time to stack the cards."

He laughed, not entirely sure she wasn't totally serious. "Keep your hands off the cards. And just in case you lose control and don't, I'll be shuffling and dealing the first hand."

"I'll still win."

"We'll see."

"And I won't have to cheat to do it," she added.

"I'm thrilled at your level of self-confidence," he assured her. "The higher you climb, the harder you'll fall."

"You wish," she hollered after him, laughter threading through her voice.

Damn, but teachers had changed a lot since his school days. If he'd had a teacher like Alice, he'd have fallen in love on the first day of school and never recovered.

Chapter Seven

The salty air had sharpened Alice's appetite and dulled her brain. She almost fell asleep waiting for Patrick to get back from Jess's with their dinner. Only a strong cup of coffee revived her. Okay, that and the prospect of beating the pants off Patrick at cards.

She hadn't been lying about her skill with a poker hand. Jess had taught her and Molly not only how to gauge their own cards, but how to read their opponents' faces. Alice could spot someone trying to bluff a mile away, while concealing her own reactions with stoic control. She'd earned a good bit of her college tuition money playing cards with unsuspecting classmates in Boston.

Because of her pretty face and naive questions, she'd suckered more than one big-talking rich boy into coughing up a healthy chunk of his allowance from home. She'd socked away several thousand dollars before word had gotten around that playing cards with Alice Newberry was as risky as investing in junk bonds. Even then there had been takers, men with big egos who'd wanted to prove that they had the card sense all the other guys had lacked. Those weekly poker games had nicely supplemented the money she earned in tips at a local bar near Boston College.

She grinned at the memory. Patrick had no idea what he was in for.

When he finally got back to the boat, he was carrying two huge sacks. He set one on the galley counter, then upended the other one in her lap. Chocolate bars spilled all over, dozens of them.

Eyes wide, she gathered up as many of them as she could reach. "Oh, my, you didn't steal all of Molly's, did you?"

He seemed to sense her ambivalence about that. "You going to give them back if I did?" he taunted.

Just the faint scent of chocolate wafting through the wrappers tempted her. "Probably not," she confessed with total honesty. When it came to chocolate, she had few scruples.

"Then it's a good thing that I drove out to the fast-mart on the highway and bought out their stock. I'd hate to bring Molly's wrath down on our heads."

"You do know I can't possibly eat all this, don't you? Or are you hoping I'll take a stab at it and wind up in some sort of diabetic coma?"

"Why would I want to do that?"

"So you can beat me at cards."

"I don't need you unconscious to win," Patrick chided. "Those candy bars are just a token of my affection. Say thank you."

She met his gaze, saw the teasing glint in his eyes and was captivated all over again. "Thank you," she said softly.

"Anytime."

The air in the tiny galley sizzled. At least it did right up until the second she caught on that charming her was his real means of attacking her concentration. If she was feeling all mushy and tender toward him, she might be distracted from playing cutthroat poker.

"It's not going to work, you know," she told him mildly, as she deliberately turned her back and ladled their soup into bowls.

"What's not going to work?"

"I'm not going to become so overwhelmed by my hormones that I can't concentrate on the cards," she said, setting the soup down in front of him.

His lips twitched slightly. "You think not?"

"I know not," she said emphatically.

"You're turning it into a challenge," he warned. "Men love challenges."

Uh-oh, she thought, recognizing the truth in that statement. Men were disgustingly predictable when it came to challenges, especially challenges uttered by a woman. She tried to regroup. "It wasn't a challenge, just a warning."

"Nice try, but I know a challenge when I hear one." He grinned as he cupped the back of her neck and held her mere inches away from his face. "And when I decide to take you up on it, you won't even see it coming."

Her stomach flipped over, even after he'd

released her. She glanced a little frantically at her watch. "It's getting late."

"Oh, no, you don't, Miss Newberry." He moved aside their untouched bowls of soup and slapped a deck of cards on the table. His gaze caught hers and held. "Ready?"

A part of Alice that had been too long dormant snapped to life. "Ready," she said, instantly revived, despite the lack of nourishment.

She leaned across the table and looked directly into his eyes. "Do your best, Devaney," she said defiantly. "It won't be good enough."

Instead of reaching for the cards, he skimmed his knuckles gently along her jaw. A half smile lifted the corners of his mouth. "We'll see."

Alice shuddered and fought the desire to lean into his touch. For the first time since she was ten years old and held her first poker hand, she had the distinct feeling that she was in way over her head in a card game.

She instinctively reached for her soup, ate several nourishing spoonfuls, then faced him with renewed determination as she looked over the cards she'd been dealt. It was the most pitiful assortment of five cards she'd ever seen, but she was used to overcoming the odds. She looked Patrick squarely in the eyes, chose two cards, when she should have dumped four, and laid them on the table.

"Two," she told him, her tone deliberately gloating.

His gaze narrowed. "Two, huh?" He dealt those and took three for himself.

Alice saw the faint twitch of his lips and knew that he'd gotten something, while her own hand was no better than it had been at the outset. Not even a pair, much less a high card to back it up. Still she tossed a few chips on the table to force Patrick to win the hand honestly.

He matched her bet. "Call."

Alice spread her woeful cards on the table, expecting to get a hearty laugh for her attempt at a bluff. As it turned out, Patrick had even less, a nine high card to her ten. She grinned and raked in the chips, noting that he didn't seem to be the least bit concerned.

"Nice bluff," he complimented her.

"You, too. You had me worried for about half a heartbeat."

She reached for the cards and shuffled. "Now I know what to look for."

"Oh?"

She grinned at him without explaining and dealt the cards. "Okay, Devaney. Time to get serious."

His gaze held hers. "Darlin', I've been serious since the minute we met."

Alice fumbled the cards and sent them flying. It was Patrick's turn to grin.

"Sorry," he apologized without a trace of sincerity in his voice. "Didn't mean to rattle you."

"You didn't," she assured him. How could he when she knew perfectly well that Patrick was never serious, not when it came to a woman? This time, though, she kept her eyes squarely on the cards.

A fat lot of good her total concentration did her, Alice thought when she'd lost three hands straight. Patrick was better than she'd expected. She was glad they were playing just for fun. Not that that had kept her competitive streak from kicking in. She still wanted to whip his butt.

"Don't get too confident, Devaney."

"I know," he said soberly. "It's just the luck of the draw."

Alice studied him. He'd sounded a little too uncharacteristically modest. "What are you up to?"

He gave her an innocent look. "Me? Nothing at all."

"You'd better not be."

"Or?" he said, barely containing a grin.

"Or you'll regret it," she said, and triumphantly spread her king-high straight on the table.

Patrick winced and folded his hand.

"Let that be a lesson to you," she gloated.

There was a devilish twinkle in his eyes when he met her gaze. "Oh, I imagine there's a great deal you could teach me, Miss Newberry."

There was no mistaking the fact that he was talking about a whole lot more than poker.

121

The evening was proving to be a lot livelier than Patrick had anticipated. Intrigued by Alice's competitive streak, he dealt, but when Alice would have picked up her cards, he placed his hand over hers. She gave him a startled look.

"Okay, enough fooling around," he declared.

"Fooling around?" she repeated, sounding breathless.

"Yeah, fooling around. It's time to get serious. What are we playing for?" he asked. "What do these chips represent? Pennies? Matchsticks?" His expression turned hopeful. "Clothes?"

Her look shot down that idea.

"Okay, you name it," he said.

"Points," she said. "Winner take all."

"And the prize?"

"When I win—"

"*If,*" he corrected.

She frowned. "Okay, if I win, you have to contact your family."

Patrick froze. Not that he expected to lose, but there was no way in hell he'd agree to those terms. "Forget it."

"You said I got to choose. Are you backing down already? You're not scared I'll beat you, are you?"

She'd caught him there. He wasn't about to let her have the upper hand, not even for a second. "Okay, then, what if I win?"

"I suppose it's only fair that you choose that," she said.

"You go to Boston with me for my brother's wedding," he said impulsively.

He knew as soon as he saw her eyes light up that he'd made a huge miscalculation. Obviously, she now saw the bet as a win-win situation for her goal of reuniting him with his family. And of course if he showed up in Boston with Alice on his arm, his brothers were going to be wearing the same gloating expression she currently had on her face.

"Done," she said at once, before he could amend the bet.

"You're sneaky," he accused her.

"No, you just subconsciously want what I want," she told him.

Patrick frowned at the suggestion that he was in any way anxious to make peace with his folks or strengthen the bond between himself and his newly found brothers.

"I made my choice six years ago. I don't regret it," he told her flatly.

"Of course you do. Whatever happened shouldn't negate all the good years you had with your family."

"Those years were a lie, and I don't regret turning my back on my parents or even on Daniel, for that matter. Maybe you had regrets about leaving home, but I don't. Don't go projecting

123

your past on me, Alice. Maybe your reasons for leaving home were less valid than mine."

Alice folded the hand of cards she held, set them facedown on the table and looked him in the eye. "I'll tell you my story if you'll tell me yours."

He saw the trap, but he was too curious to deny himself the chance to learn more about her. "Okay. You first. Why did you take off the minute you got out of high school?"

"Because I was determined not to be trapped here the way all of the women in my family had been for generations. They grew up, finished high school, got married to a local fisherman and stayed home with the kids. Many of them lost their husbands to the sea. It was a hard life, even for those who didn't lose their husbands, and I wanted more than that. I wanted my own identity, my own career to fall back on."

Patrick didn't see why that should have caused such a rift that she'd never seen her folks again. "What am I missing? That doesn't sound so awful."

She sighed heavily. "It shouldn't have been, not in this day and age, but my parents were very traditional. They saw my decision as a reflection on their choices. They said if what they'd given me wasn't good enough, then I should just get out and see how hard it was to make it on my own. So that's what I did. I left. I had just enough money to get to Boston and spend a few nights in a boarding house near Boston College. I had no money for classes and very little for food. I was lucky, though. I got a job after a few days, and it paid the bills with a little extra. Playing poker added to my savings, but even so it took me a year to save enough to start taking classes. I was twenty-two when I graduated and I've been teaching now for four years, three in Boston, one here."

"Good for you! You should be proud of yourself."

"I was. I *am*," she said with a touch of defiance.

He studied her intently, trying to figure out why she sounded as if she still felt she had something to prove. "In all that time your parents never contacted you?"

She shook her head, her expression unbearably sad. "Not once. I invited them to my graduation, but they didn't even reply. I heard after they died that my mother wanted to come, but my father refused and she wouldn't go against his wishes even then."

"I'm sorry."

There were unshed tears in her eyes when she looked at him. "It was all so silly. I was too stubborn and they had too much pride. If only any one of us had reached out, maybe we could have worked things out."

"Why didn't you?"

"I did reach out. I sent that invitation. I thought it was a gesture, but I don't know, maybe they saw it as a slap in the face, as me trying to show them how I'd done what I set out to do to spite them. And after that, I suppose their refusal to come to my graduation was one more blow. I felt as if I'd been rejected again. I'd been thinking about them a lot in the months before they died. I almost came home several times. I thought maybe if I just showed up it would be easier." She met his gaze. "Then it was too late. I'll blame myself forever for waiting too long."

"You couldn't have known that there wouldn't be years and years to mend fences."

"No, but it proved that things shouldn't be allowed to fester. We never know how long we have. The bitterness between us will be on my conscience forever."

Patrick looked away, thinking about the bitterness and anger and blame between him and his parents. As far as he could see, there was still no comparison between what they had done and what Alice's parents had done. The Newberrys had never abandoned three little boys. The Devaneys had, and they'd done it without once looking back. In his eyes that was unforgivable.

"You promised to tell me about your split with your family," Alice reminded him.

He had and he regretted it, but he wasn't going to renege on his promise. "It's an ugly story," he warned her.

"I still want to hear it."

He nodded. "Then I need a drink. You want any-thing?"

She shook her head as he poured a shot of Irish whiskey into a glass and drank it down. It burned his throat and made his eyes water, but a moment later he could feel the warmth stealing through him. It was a comforting sensation, which was one reason he rarely touched the stuff. It would be too easy to get lost in it.

"Okay," he began. "Here's the short version. Unbeknownst to me or Daniel, my parents had three sons before they had us. You met them the other night—Ryan, Sean and Michael. I guess on some level we knew about them, because we were two when things fell apart. We had to have been aware that we had big brothers, but kids forget. They're adaptable at that age. At any rate, our folks just picked up stakes and moved to Maine with Daniel and me." He looked directly into her eyes, then added so there could be no mistake about what he was saying, "They left their other sons behind."

Alice stared at him, evidently not compre-hending . . . or not wanting to. "What do you mean they left them? With friends? Another family?"

He shook his head. "They left them for Social Services to deal with. Ryan and Sean came home from school, and the rest of us were gone. Michael was with a baby-sitter."

"My God!" she whispered.

127

"It gets worse," Patrick told her, needing her to understand the full extent of his parents' treachery. "They never once checked on them. Ryan, Sean and Michael were separated. They were placed in foster care. Michael says his family was terrific and Sean's was okay, but Ryan was understandably angry and hard to deal with. He bounced from home to home. Because of the way my parents left, there was no way any of them could be put up for adoption, not with the laws on the books then. Instead, they led makeshift lives with makeshift families."

"How awful for them," Alice said, obviously shaken. "And you had no idea?"

"Not until I was eighteen. Daniel found some old photos hidden in the attic. We asked our folks about them. They admitted that they'd left their oldest three sons behind in Boston when they moved here, that they had no idea how they were. Maybe if they'd at least given permission for them to be adopted, I could forgive them, but to leave them in limbo like that . . . how could they?"

He met her gaze. "They refused to explain what they'd done. In fact, they acted as if we didn't even have the right to ask. Daniel stuck around. He's still hoping for an explanation, I guess. As for me, I will never forgive what they've done. There isn't an explanation they can give that would make what they did okay. I keep trying to put myself in my brothers' shoes on that day, coming back to an empty apartment, finding out that they'd been left behind. They must have been terrified. It makes me sick to my stomach just thinking about it."

"Your parents must have been desperate to do such a thing," Alice said, trying to explain away the inexplicable.

"Don't defend them to me!" Patrick said. "Put yourself in my brothers' shoes. Ryan was barely nine, the others even younger, and they were abandoned by their family, while Daniel and I were chosen to go with our parents. My God, what kind of selfish, cruel person does that to three little boys?"

"Only someone who's desperate," Alice insisted again. "Someone who can't see any other way out."

"They were adults. They had a responsibility to their children to find another way out," he said, his tone harsh. He sighed heavily. "For the longest time after Daniel and I found out, I dreamed about them. I kept seeing their faces, imagining them crying. I wanted to look for them, but I was scared."

"Scared of what?"

"That they'd hate me, or at the very least, resent me for being chosen to go with our parents." He regarded her with a sense of wonder. "The amazing thing is that they don't. They came here wanting answers, not revenge."

"Doesn't that tell you something?" Alice asked.

"That they're incredible men to have survived what our folks did to them," he said at once. "But I still don't feel right being around them. I feel as if I was given something they should have had, something they were entitled to—a secure home, parental love."

"It didn't seem to me as if they begrudge you that," Alice said.

"They don't," he admitted. "Like I said, they're better men than I am."

"No, they're not," she said fiercely.

Patrick grinned at her. "You don't know me well enough to be so quick to jump to my defense."

"Of course I do," she said. "Have you even been listening to yourself? You're not just upset with your parents because they lied to you and Daniel, you're filled with compassion and righteous indignation on behalf of brothers you didn't even remember. You're as connected to them as if you'd spent a lifetime together."

She gave him a sly look. "The only thing that might make you an even better man would be putting out the effort to make things right."

"Don't even go there," Patrick warned. "I'm not going to organize some big reconciliation between them and my folks. I don't ever want to see my parents again. The only reason I'm even going to Boston for this wedding is because it seems to mean a lot to Michael, Sean and Ryan. After that, if they want to track down Daniel and our parents, it's up to them. I want no part of it."

He expected her to deliver another lecture, but instead she merely said quietly, "Maybe you'll change your mind."

"I won't. If you're counting on that, you're going to be disappointed."

"We'll see."

"It's not going to happen, Alice."

"Whatever you say."

"Don't patronize me, dammit!"

She gave him a serene smile that almost sent him over the edge. He barely resisted the urge to pound the table to emphasize his point. Instead he picked up his cards and looked them over, relieved to see that he had a full house working. He tossed one card and waited for Alice to deal him another. After a long look, she finally did just that without further comment.

Patrick took that hand and then the next, but then Alice went on a winning streak that caught him by surprise. When she finally yawned and called it a night, she'd accumulated twenty points to his eighteen.

To her credit, she didn't gloat. Nor did she push overly hard for the reconciliation he'd declared wasn't going to happen.

"We'll talk about you paying up on our bet when you get back from Boston," she said mildly as she headed for the deck. Then she smiled up at him.

"Of course, if you wanted to smooth things out with your brothers while you're there, then there won't even be anything to talk about except getting you back together with your folks."

Despite his annoyance, Patrick couldn't help admiring her tenacity. "We'll see," he said, snagging her hand and pulling her toward him. He brushed an errant curl away from her face and let his hand linger. "You're quite the little nag, aren't you?"

She grinned, obviously not taking offense. "You have no idea."

"Proud of it, too," he concluded.

"You bet, especially when the cause is such a good one."

"What if I were to threaten to kiss you each and every time you brought up the subject?" he inquired curiously.

She laughed at that. "Then you'd just be making it a whole lot more interesting."

He studied her with surprise. "Really?"

"Really," she said, keeping her expression serious, even though her eyes were twinkling merrily. "Good night, Patrick."

She pulled away and stepped onto the dock. "I can't wait to hear all about Boston."

"You could still come with me," he called after her.

"I don't think so. I think I'll just trust you to do the right thing."

He watched her until she reached her car and drove away, then sighed. He really, really hated having someone count on him to do the right thing. In this situation he wasn't even sure what the right thing was.

Chapter Eight

By Monday morning, Alice was already feeling restless and at loose ends. Spring break stretched out ahead of her like a prison sentence, rather than a relaxing vacation. Even though keeping up with a classroom full of five-year-olds was stressful, having time to herself with nothing to do but think about the past was worse. And now she had her conflicting emotions over Patrick to add into the mix. She would have given almost anything to have Ricky Foster around to give her a run for her money and keep her mind occupied.

Since she couldn't have that distraction, she opted for going to Jess's to see Molly. Molly was always good for some lively conversation, and she always knew the latest gossip in Widow's Cove.

Alice knew the second she walked through the door and saw her friend's face light up that she'd probably made a mistake.

"Over here," Molly ordered, gesturing toward a secluded booth. She brought the coffeepot and two cups with her. "Talk," she said as she poured the coffee.

Alice gave her a disgruntled look. "Any particular topic?"

"Don't even try to pretend you don't know what I'm asking about," Molly retorted. "You and Patrick. How's that going?"

Since Molly was unlikely to drop the subject, Alice concluded that the smart thing would be to turn Molly's fascination to her advantage. "What do you know about Patrick's brother Daniel?"

Molly made a face. "A pompous, self-righteous jerk," she said succinctly. She looked as if she wanted to say a lot more, but she didn't.

Alice's gaze narrowed. The description sounded more personal than objective. "Okay, spill it, Molly. What did he ever do to you?"

"Nothing," Molly said a little too quickly.

"Come on, Molly, tell the truth. You don't say things like that about someone unless they've done you wrong."

"Not me. Patrick," Molly insisted.

Alice studied her skeptically. "And that's it? You don't like him, because he what? Took Patrick at his word and left him alone?"

"Pretty much." She said it easily enough, but she wouldn't meet Alice's gaze.

"I'm not buying it," Alice said. "If that's all it was, you'd be moving heaven and earth to patch things up between them."

"The same way you are?" Molly asked testily.

"Exactly."

"Maybe I'm just not as inclined to meddle in something that's none of my business."

Alice gave her a wry look. "Since when?"

"Since it's Daniel Devaney we're talking about,

if you must know. The man gets on my nerves, that's all."

"Oh, really?" Alice thought she was finally getting a lot closer to the truth. "It's only a tiny little leap from getting on your nerves to getting under your skin. Do you have a thing for Daniel?"

Molly looked as scandalized as if Alice had accused her of stealing from the poor. "Don't be absurd. The man would never give me a second look, and I don't waste my time pining for idiots."

Now there was a telling comment, Alice thought. She wondered if Molly realized she'd all but admitted to having feelings, even if they were feelings she was fighting.

"Is he as handsome as his brother?"

"They're identical twins," Molly retorted, then rested her chin on her hand and leveled a speculative look straight into Alice's eyes. "You tell me, does that make him handsome?"

Alice couldn't seem to prevent the blush that crept into her cheeks. If she expected total honesty from her friend, then she needed to repay it in kind. "It does in my book," she admitted.

Molly sat back with a satisfied look. "I thought so. How far has it gone?"

"It hasn't gone anywhere. We went out on his boat on Saturday, had dinner and played cards. Just a relaxing day. Nothing more."

"You were down in that cozy little place of his below deck till well after midnight and all you did was play cards? I am very disappointed in you," Molly chided.

Alice regarded Molly curiously. "How did you know I was there past midnight?"

"I wasn't down there peering in the portholes, if that's what you're thinking," Molly retorted. "Your car was still there when I closed up here. If you didn't want me to notice it, you should have parked someplace else or left earlier. The point is, you were with the man and wasting time on cards." Her expression brightened. "Was it strip poker at least?"

"No, it was not strip poker!" Alice said with feigned indignation. "As a matter of fact, the stakes were much higher."

"Oh, really? Maybe you didn't let me down after all. What were they?"

"If I won—which I did—he would make peace with his family."

Molly stared, obviously shocked. "Patrick agreed to that?"

Alice grinned. "He didn't expect to lose."

"You did tell him that Jess taught you to play poker didn't you?"

"I did, and apparently he wasn't overly impressed."

"Foolish man."

Alice shrugged. "His gullibility served my purposes very nicely."

"So now you're trying to figure out how to bring

about this reconciliation?" Molly concluded. "Is that why you were asking about Daniel? You think he's the obvious link?"

"You disagree?"

"Let's just say I wouldn't turn to Daniel if my life were on the line, but that's just me."

Alice grinned. "Interesting. All that vehement protesting and your cheeks are bright pink."

"Don't make too much of that. The man infuriates me."

"My point exactly," Alice said. "I think I'll see what I can do about hooking up with Daniel Devaney while I'm on break from school."

"Patrick won't thank you for interfering in his life," Molly warned.

"Sometimes you just have to do what you think is best and to hell with the consequences for yourself," Alice said.

"You don't care if Patrick is furious with you?"

"I'd prefer it if he weren't," Alice admitted. "But I'm willing to take the risk."

"You're a braver woman that I am," Molly said, regarding her with admiration. "Just don't expect too much from Daniel. And don't go dragging him down here for this big reconciliation. I don't want him on the property."

She sounded dead serious. Alice studied her more closely. "How did he let you down, Molly?"

"I never said he let me down. I believe I said he was a pompous, self-righteous jerk."

"Because he let you down," Alice repeated confidently. "That just gives me one more thing to straighten out."

"I do not want to be your spring break project!" Molly shouted after her as she headed for the door. "I doubt that Patrick does, either."

"That's the problem with having a friend who has good intentions and time on her hands," Alice called back. "We just go on about the business of doing our good deeds, anyway."

Patrick heard all about Alice's visit to Jess's the second he crossed the bar's threshold on Monday evening. Molly couldn't shut up about it.

"So what?" he asked, when he could finally get a word in. "It's not as if Daniel is going to come roaring over here to make peace just because Alice pesters him to do it. He knows better, at least where I'm concerned. What about you? You interested in making peace with my brother?"

"When hell freezes over," Molly said fiercely.

Patrick grinned. "You might want to tone down that response. It tends to give away the fact that down deep, you still have the hots for the man."

"I most certainly do not," Molly said. "And you, of all people, know exactly why that is."

Patrick sobered at once. "I do know, Molly, and you'll get no argument from me. He treated you badly, and you have every reason to hate him."

"To say nothing of the way he stood behind your

folks rather than you," she said. "I can't forgive him for that, either."

"Leave me out of it. Daniel and I can wrestle with our issues. You don't have to take on my battle. And I won't hold it against you if you were ever to decide to give him another chance."

"I won't," Molly said flatly. "I'd say he's shown us both his true character, wouldn't you? Who needs it?"

Just then she glanced toward the door, and her expression turned sour. "Don't look now, but our meddling friend is back to report in on her day's adventures."

Patrick swiveled his stool around to see Alice marching toward them with a determined glint in her eyes. She looked as if she were returning from battle, though he couldn't quite read whether she'd been victorious.

"Have a busy day?" he inquired lightly.

"As a matter of fact, I did," she told him. "I went to see your brother."

"So I heard," he said, keeping his tone neutral.

Alice frowned at Molly. "You blabbed?"

"Of course, I told him," Molly said without regret. "He had a right to know."

"I suppose," Alice conceded.

Despite his irritation, Patrick was curious. "How'd it go?"

"He told me to mind my own damn business," she said indignantly. "And I am quoting him precisely."

140

Molly chuckled. "That's our Daniel. Never did mince words. Despite his tendency to want to keep the peace, the man has the diplomatic skills of Attila the Hun."

"Funny, he said pretty much the same thing about you," Alice retorted. "What the devil went on between you two, anyway? I have a feeling if I'd never mentioned your name, I might have gotten further."

"None of your business," Molly retorted.

Alice sighed. "I'm just trying to help."

Patrick understood that her heart was in the right place, but he'd tried to tell her not to waste her energy fighting his battles. Molly had apparently told her the same thing. "Leave it alone, Alice. Things are the way they're meant to be."

"Life is not meant to be lived like this. Families shouldn't be split up," she argued.

"Tell that to my folks," he said. "They're the ones responsible."

"Way back then, when they left Boston, yes," she agreed. "But you've only made it worse, and they've all let you get away with it."

"Which only means that we're all content with the status quo," he pointed out. "Leave it be." He tucked a finger under her chin and forced her to meet his gaze. "How about I buy you dinner?"

"I'm not hungry," she said, her expression glum.

"A drink, then?"

"Sure." She looked at Molly. "A diet soda, please."

Patrick grinned. "Big drinker, huh?"

"I know better than to drink anything else on an empty stomach."

"Then let me buy you dinner," he repeated. "The special's pork chops."

"Not interested," she insisted.

Patrick turned to Molly. "Make it one special, then. We'll be in that booth over there."

Molly frowned at him. "I don't get it, Patrick. Why aren't you more upset that Alice went meddling where she didn't belong?"

"Because he was secretly hoping I'd fix things," Alice said.

Patrick frowned at her. "No, because it's no big deal. I knew how it was going to turn out before Alice ever went traipsing after Daniel. So did you, Molly. You could have saved your breath trying to stop her. There was nothing to worry about."

"I wasn't worried. I was annoyed," Molly said. "I didn't like the idea earlier, and I'm no happier about it now." She scowled at Alice. "No more meddling on my behalf, okay? Promise me."

"Fine. I promise," Alice said.

She looked so dejected Patrick almost felt sorry for her. She'd obviously wanted to do something helpful, and she'd only been slapped down from all directions for her efforts.

"Come on," he said, steering her over to a booth.

When she was settled across from him, he met her gaze. "Come on, Alice, cheer up. You tried. It didn't work out. I'm not unhappy about that. Molly is definitely not unhappy about it. You shouldn't be, either."

"Why is everyone being so stubborn?"

He grinned at the plaintive note in her voice. "I can't speak for Molly, but as for Daniel and me, we're Devaneys. It comes with the genes."

"More's the pity," she muttered.

"Forget about it. Come to Boston with me this weekend. We'll have some fun, go to the wedding and you'll see that none of this matters in the greater scheme of things."

"I don't think so," she said as indignantly as if he'd suggested they go skinny-dipping in broad daylight. "I won our bet. I can't go to Boston."

He chuckled. "We can pretend I won. Or we can play one hand of poker right here and now, winner take all."

She shook her head. "I don't think so. I've already bumped up against two stubborn Devaneys. I'm not sure I could handle a whole crowd of them."

He laughed at that. "That makes two of us. Think of it this way—you coming along would be a mission of mercy."

She finally grinned at that. "Nice try, Devaney, but you're not going to get me by playing on my sympathy. I will take those pork chops, though."

She glanced at Molly, who was across the room taking in the scene with obvious fascination. "With mashed potatoes and gravy, please."

Patrick winked at Molly. "Give the lady whatever she wants."

"Naturally," Molly said. "Around here we aim to please our customers."

Alice gave her a sour look. "Then you can lay off all the I-told-you-so's that are on the tip of your tongue."

Molly grinned. "I'm not sure I can go that far."

"Try," Alice said. "Otherwise, I might be tempted to take one more stab at getting Daniel to listen to me."

"Then by all means, Molly, keep your mouth shut," Patrick said fervently. Given his own inability to resist Alice, he doubted his brother could withstand another persuasive onslaught, and the last thing he wanted was for Alice to manage to drag Daniel over here where he'd only stir up a lot of old issues for Patrick—and for Molly.

Patrick had second and then third thoughts on the drive down to Boston. Michael's wedding was just about the last place on earth he wanted to be, but he'd made his brothers a promise and he didn't intend to break it. If having him there made up for some of the old hurts inflicted by their folks, then it was the least he could do.

He drove straight to his oldest brother's pub,

144

then stood outside Ryan's Place trying to work up the courage to go in. At that moment he regretted, more than he could say, not trying harder to talk Alice into coming with him. Staring through the glass, he was grateful that the pub was packed. He doubted Ryan would have much time for him. He could say hello and head to his hotel, then try to regroup in time for tomorrow's wedding. With any luck there would be so much commotion at the wedding no one would even notice he was there.

When Patrick finally walked into the bar, Ryan spotted him at once and his face lit up.

"You're just in time," he called out. "I could use some help back here. You any good at pouring drinks?"

"I've filled in for Molly a time or two," Patrick admitted, relieved to have something to do. "Nice place you've got here. You always this busy?"

"It's a Friday night. We have music starting in an hour. If you think it's packed now, just wait."

"Aren't you supposed to be going to the rehearsal dinner in a little while?"

"Maggie and Caitlyn will stand in for me," Ryan said. "Besides, I wanted to spend some time with you. Since you turned down the invitation to the dinner, I figured this would be my best chance. Michael understands. He knows what it's like around here on the weekends. That's one reason he's having a morning wedding, so the reception will be over with in time for me to get back here tomorrow night." He grinned. "That and the fact that he's anxious to get Kelly on a plane to head for their honeymoon. They're going to some Caribbean island."

"Sounds romantic," Patrick said.

"Our brother has a romantic streak. I guess all the Devaneys do, once some woman manages to knock down the walls we've built around our hearts. What about you? Anyone ever gotten through your defenses?"

Patrick's heart thudded dully at the first volley from his big brother. Because Ryan was heading down a path Patrick didn't want to explore, he decided to turn the tables.

"Tell me about Maggie and your daughter," he said. "You have any pictures around here?"

Ryan regarded him with a knowing expression but didn't call him on the deliberate distraction. "Upstairs in our old apartment, where you'll be staying," Ryan said. "If you want to take your stuff on up and get settled, I can handle things here for a bit."

Grateful for the excuse to have a few minutes to himself, Patrick grabbed his suitcase and headed upstairs. He closed the door to the apartment behind him and drew in a deep breath. He felt as if he'd fallen into the middle of someone else's life. He was in a strange city, a strange apartment and trying to pretend that his own brother wasn't a complete stranger.

He set his one bag inside the door and flipped on the lights. The apartment was cozy and filled with the kind of touches only a woman could have put there. There were even fresh flowers in a vase on the coffee table and a welcoming note from Maggie propped against a family photo. He stared at the picture and found himself grinning.

Ryan looked as if he couldn't tear his gaze away from the two girls in his life. If he'd had to guess, he would say the photo had been taken in Ireland. The landscape was as green as could be, and they were standing on a rocky cliff overlooking the sea. A woman—obviously his beloved Maggie—had long red hair that had been caught by the breeze and a serene expression on her face. A pint-size miniature of her was wearing a bright-pink sweater, emerald-green pants and bright-yellow sneakers. She was obviously a child who had her own sense of fashion. And it was equally evident that the two adults doted on her. Patrick envied them the closeness that shone on their faces.

Turning his back on that momentary pang of envy, he quickly shut the door and went back downstairs.

Ryan looked up from the ale he was pouring and gave him a sharp look. "Everything okay?"

"Fine," Patrick said.

"You find everything you needed upstairs?"

"Yes," he said. He'd found everything he needed, along with something he hadn't even realized he wanted . . . evidence of what a thoroughly happy family was supposed to look like.

"You sure you don't mind if I put you to work?" Ryan asked.

"Not at all," Patrick said and meant it. It felt good to be needed. "Just tell me what to do."

Ryan pointed out where the various bottles of whiskey and wine were kept, showed him what beer and ales were on tap, then left him to it.

Patrick immediately fell into the rhythm of the pub, making chitchat with the waitresses, flirting just a little with the women who sat at the bar, then letting the familiar Irish songs wash over him in waves of nostalgia. Connor Devaney had played those same songs until the tapes wore out and had to be replaced by CDs. Not a day had gone by that he and Daniel hadn't felt ties to a land they'd never seen. And more than once, on a visit to Jess's, Connor had ended the evening with his own powerful voice singing "Danny Boy," as Patrick and Daniel sat on his knees. Now Connor never crossed the threshold of his old haunt, because Patrick had made it his own and all but declared it off-limits.

Funny how he'd pushed memories like that from his head during the past few years. He hadn't wanted to remember any of the good times, because he'd felt that they'd come at the expense of his brothers. Tonight, though, he could listen to that old familiar music without guilt. In a way, he owed Ryan for that, for giving him back a piece of himself.

Once the band finished for the night, the pub emptied out quickly. Ryan drew in a deep breath and gave Patrick a grin.

"Not bad, bro. I appreciate the help."

Patrick moved to a bar stool and sank onto it. "I thought fishing was hard work, but this was a thousand times worse."

"You said you'd worked at Jess's."

"Jess's is never packed like this. It's half the size, so even on a crowded night there's time to breathe."

"You want to head upstairs and get some sleep?" Ryan asked. "If you're exhausted at the wedding, I'll catch hell for it."

Patrick almost took him up on it. It would be better than sticking around for the questions that had been on the tip of his brother's tongue all evening. But that would be the cowardly way out, and Patrick had always prided himself on facing things.

"If you don't mind, I think I'd like a pint of that ale before I go up," he told Ryan.

"Coming right up," his brother said. He poured one for each of them, then rounded the bar and sat next to Patrick. "Now that you've had some time to think about it, how do you feel about

Sean, Michael and me showing up last week?"

"To be honest, I can't quite get over it. I'm still feeling a little off-kilter, the same way I did when I first found out we'd run out on you." He looked Ryan in the eye. "And I can't believe you're not angrier."

"Believe me, I spent a lot of years being furious," Ryan said. "I caused a lot of trouble for a lot of foster families before I was finally old enough to go out on my own. And then I came damn close to landing in jail, but a good friend got me back on track. You'll meet Father Francis at the wedding tomorrow. The man's a saint to have put up with me. I owe him for all of this. He made me see what I could be."

"Obviously, he knew what he was talking about," Patrick said. "You've made a nice life for yourself here. The pub's really something."

"It's even better now that I've let Maggie into my life. Don't tell her I said this, but she's given this place the heart it lacked. It was a well-run pub before, but now it has her warmth, to say nothing of her clever way with a dollar. We've never done better." He grinned. "And we've another baby on the way, a boy this time."

"Congratulations!" Patrick said, feeling another surprising twinge of envy.

"You'll meet someone one of these days," Ryan told him, then gave him a sly look. "Or perhaps you already have."

"If you're talking about Alice, I told you I barely know her."

"Sometimes it doesn't take that long, when it's the right woman."

"She's a meddler," Patrick complained, feeling disloyal even as he said it. He knew better than anyone that Alice had a good heart, even if her attempts to help were misguided.

Ryan laughed. "Maybe so, but I imagine my Maggie could still give her lessons. Meddling's not a crime, if it's done for the right reasons. Not that I would have said that a few years back, with Father Francis and then Maggie thinking they knew what was best for me."

"You didn't appreciate what they were trying to do at the time?"

"Of course not, but I got over it eventually. If you're smart, you will, too. There's nothing like the love of a good woman to fill a man's heart and make his life worth living."

Patrick regarded him sadly. "Do you suppose our folks felt that way once?"

"They're still together, aren't they?" Ryan asked. "That says something. I'm not saying I understand or forgive what they did to Sean, Michael and me, or even to you and Daniel by keeping you in the dark, but they've stuck together. It takes a strong glue to do that, and the only one I know that powerful is love."

151

Patrick thought of the years when he'd thought the same. "I suppose."

"Weren't there happy times for all of you?" Ryan asked. "I'd hate to think that they caused such misery for the rest of us without finding some happiness with you and Daniel."

"How can there be any real happiness when it's based on a lie?" Patrick asked.

"Come on, Patrick," Ryan chided, "be honest. Were there good times? Was there laughter?"

Patrick wanted to deny it, but he couldn't. "Yes." He studied his brother curiously. "Don't you begrudge us that?"

Ryan took his time answering, clearly giving his reply some serous thought. "No, I don't think so. I think it would be unbearably sad if you had all been miserable, too."

"You have a generous heart," Patrick told him with sincerity. "More generous than mine. I doubt I'll ever forgive them for stealing so many years from all of us."

"We have the here and now," Ryan said. "In the end, that's all any of us have. The past is over, if not forgotten, and hating's a waste of time and energy. The future's out there, and the way it goes depends on what we do today. Maggie taught me that."

Patrick sipped his ale, then admitted, "Alice said something very much like it."

"A wise woman," Ryan said. "You should listen

to her. I've been happier since I put aside my anger. I've been happier yet since I started paying attention to my wife. She sees things with a clarity that I can't. She's been a blessing, no doubt about it."

Was Alice the same sort of blessing? Patrick wondered. It was too soon to tell. But at that moment he couldn't wait to get back to Maine to find out.

Chapter Nine

Alice gave her tiny cottage a thorough spring housecleaning, just to keep herself from thinking too much about what might be going on in Boston between Patrick and his brothers. She also needed to avoid her natural inclination to try to patch things up between him and Daniel and their parents. She'd promised to stay out of that and she intended to keep her word . . . unless, of course, she saw that they were making no progress on their own. Then she'd have a duty to step in, whether anyone appreciated her efforts or not.

For the most part, she managed to keep her thoughts of Patrick at bay as she washed windows till they glistened, scrubbed floors till they shone and dusted every single knickknack and surface throughout the four-room house. She lingered for several minutes over the photo of her parents taken during a family outing just a few months before her high school graduation. At that point they'd had no idea that she intended to leave Maine and go to college in Boston. She'd still been their cherished daughter.

"Oh, Mama," she whispered. "I never meant to hurt the two of you. I just needed you to respect my choice. If only you had. . . ."

But they hadn't, and from the moment she'd announced her intentions, their world had been shattered. It wasn't as if she'd sprung it on them, either. She'd made no secret of applying to colleges, but they'd assumed she either wouldn't get in or would change her mind and stay right here in Widow's Cove, content to work as a clerk in some store until the right man came along.

Sighing at how naive they'd all been, she put the photo back on its shelf and went on with her cleaning.

With a warm breeze billowing the curtains and filling the house with fresh air, Alice finally collapsed into her favorite chintz-covered easy chair with a cup of tea and a slice of freshly baked apple pie. Before she took so much as a sip of tea, she closed her eyes and breathed deeply, feeling the tense muscles in her neck and shoulders finally ease. There was nothing like exhausting physical work to sweep the cobwebs from the mind, she thought as the faint sounds of a classical music station drifted from the radio.

Just when she felt herself beginning to unwind, the jarring sound of the phone startled her. She glanced at the clock and was surprised to see that the entire day had slipped away from her. It was after seven. Little wonder she was tired and hungry. She'd missed dinner completely in her frenzy to keep occupied.

The phone continued its insistent ringing as she conducted a frantic search for the portable receiver she'd left somewhere. She finally found it under a pile of throw pillows on the sofa. They'd done little to muffle the sound.

"Yes, hello," she said finally.

"What took so long? Were you asleep?"

"Patrick?" She felt her mouth curve into a smile at the unexpected sound of his voice.

"Yes."

"You're not back from Boston already, are you?"

"Nope. The reception ended a little while ago. I'm on my way back to Ryan's and decided to stop at a pay phone and give you a call."

Something inside her melted at that. "How was the wedding?"

"Okay, I suppose. They wrote their own vows. I guess Kelly played a big part in getting Michael back on his feet after he was shot. He talked about how much he owed her and how without her he wouldn't be standing at all, much less standing by her side. There wasn't a dry eye left in the church when they were finished."

"Even yours?"

"Yes, even mine," he said. "I'm not that cynical and jaded that a touching story can't get to me."

"Glad to hear it. So, tell me, what's your brother's bride like?"

"Beautiful, feisty—pretty much like the other two Devaney brides. Deanna has Sean wrapped around her finger. And Maggie, Ryan's wife, is really something. You'd like her. She's already nagging me about spending more time down here."

Alice felt her heart climb into her throat. What was there for Patrick in Maine, really? In Boston a whole new family awaited him. "What did you tell her? Would you consider moving down there?" she asked, trying to keep any hint of dismay out of her voice.

"Why would I do that?" he asked, sounding genuinely puzzled by the question.

"So you could spend more time with your brothers and their families," she explained.

"No way. Widow's Cove is my home. I love fishing. And lately, well, let's just say that I'm highly motivated to get back home."

"Why is that?" she asked, hardly daring to believe the implication that it had something to do with her.

"Well, you see, there's this schoolteacher," he began, lowering his voice to a seductive purr.

"Oh?"

"I can't seem to get her out of my head," he said. "She's thoroughly exasperating. She meddles. She cheats at poker."

"I do not cheat!"

"Oh, did you think I was talking about you?" he asked.

She could almost hear the smile in his voice. "Then this anonymous teacher has gotten to you, is that what you're saying?"

"I believe she has."

"Fascinating," she said, an unfamiliar warmth stealing through her at his admission.

"Yeah, it's definitely fascinating," he said. "I suppose we need to talk some more about that when I get back."

In Alice's opinion, talking was sometimes highly overrated, especially when you knew how cautious the other person was likely to be. Maybe she'd do something wildly impetuous to jump-start things, now that he'd given her a proper signal.

"What have you been up to today?" Patrick asked.

"Nothing much, just some spring cleaning."

"Meaning you probably turned the place upside down and inside out to scrub every square inch of it," he teased.

"Pretty much."

"Then I imagine you're tired. I should let you get some rest."

"And you should get back to your brother's," she said. "I'm glad you called, though. And I'm especially happy that things are going so well for you and your brothers. It must feel pretty amazing to have them back in your life."

"Better than I expected," he conceded.

"Have you talked about Daniel and your folks at all?"

"A bit with Ryan, but I imagine the subject will come up with the others before I manage to get out of town. I think everyone's waiting till after the wedding to get into anything else. I don't think they want anything to spoil this day for Michael and Kelly. Now that they've left on their honeymoon, I suspect the kid gloves will come off and we'll get down to the hard stuff."

"Have you thought about what you're going to do when the subject does come up?"

"I've already made my position plain. I'll tell them where to find Daniel and the folks, but I'm out when it comes to any grand reunion."

"Oh, Patrick," Alice whispered sadly.

"I've told you before that that's the way it has to be. I won't change my mind," he said tightly. "Good night, Alice. I'll see you when I get back."

Filled with regret over having spoiled his good mood, she murmured a goodbye, then slowly hung up the phone. As she did, she realized that her palms were sweating and her pulse was racing. How long had it been since the simple sound of a man's voice had had the power to make her react like that? And why did it have to be Patrick Devaney, of all men, who'd reminded her of what it felt like to be a desirable woman? How could she possibly allow herself to fall for a man who was so clearly destined to make the very same mistakes she'd spend the rest of her life regretting?

Patrick's trip to Boston went better than he'd anticipated. Maybe if they lived closer, he could be friends with these men who were his brothers and

159

with their wives. He was already crazy about his irrepressible niece, Caitlyn, and his too-wise-for-his-years nephew, Kevin.

But as he'd told Alice so emphatically, he wanted no part in their plan to get in touch with Daniel or their folks. He understood their need to make contact and find answers, but he already knew all he needed to know. He'd given his brothers an address and a phone number and left it at that. From here on out, they were on their own.

There had been no mistaking the disappointment in Alice's voice when he'd explained his stance to her. His brothers, however, had seemed to understand. They were going into this final stage of their search for answers with their guard up and their own share of anger.

"We'll let you know when we're coming up to Maine," Ryan had promised him.

"And we expect to spend time with you," Maggie had added firmly. "The trip won't be just about your folks and Daniel. We don't intend to lose touch now that we've found you. You have family, Patrick. We won't ever turn our backs on you."

Patrick had heard the total sincerity and love behind her words with a sense of amazement. Maggie and all of her huge family of O'Briens had welcomed him into their hearts. Michael's foster family, the Havilceks, had done the same. Though Patrick had lost the three most important people in his life when he'd left home, he suddenly found himself surrounded once again by family. It wasn't as suffocating as he'd feared it might be. Instead, it had healed a part of his heart that he'd been pretending wasn't broken.

Not that he entirely trusted this glow of rediscovery to last forever. Right now he was new to all of them, but in time they would settle into their own lives down in Boston and leave him to his. When that happened, he knew he would be lonelier than ever.

Still, he felt surprisingly good about the weekend he'd shared with his brothers. Their talks had reminded him of the many nights he and Daniel had stayed up as boys, talking over their day, discussing girls, planning strategy for the football field, where they excelled. He'd missed that kind of camaraderie.

It was late Sunday evening when he opened the gate on his dock and headed toward his boat. A faint whiff of perfume on the salt breeze had him smiling.

"Somebody's trespassing again," he said loudly enough to be heard. "Maybe I should call the police."

"Go right ahead," Alice said tartly. "But you'll miss the effect of finding me naked in your bed."

Patrick nearly choked. "Excuse me?" Surely she wasn't really naked . . . or in his bed, but the image was going to drive him wild for a long time to come. That she'd even suggested such a thing was enough to have his heart thundering and his pulse racing.

On the off chance that she was more daring than he'd realized, he all but ran to the boat. He found her standing on deck, wrapped in a blanket. He stared at her suspiciously. "Do you have anything on under there?"

"Maybe," she said with a coy smile. "Maybe not."

Patrick groaned. "What are you trying to do to me?"

"Isn't that obvious?"

"Drive me crazy? Seduce me?"

Her lips curved into a smile. "Both. I know how you have a tendency to overthink things, so I thought I'd be here to welcome you home. I couldn't resist. Do you mind?"

He studied her, from her wind-tousled hair to the pink in her cheeks, then searched her face. There was the faintest hint of uncertainty in her eyes. So Alice wasn't nearly as used to being brazen as she wanted him to believe. That charmed him all the more, even as it scared the daylights out of him. He'd intended to take things slowly, to be sensible.

"Quite a homecoming," he murmured, brushing a stray curl from her cheek. He felt her skin heat at the contact.

"Glad you appreciate it, because I'm actually freezing."

He skimmed a finger along the bare skin at the edge of the blanket. His touch raised goose bumps. "So I see. Your skin feels warm enough, though."

"Keep that up and you'll have me on fire," she said, a hitch in her voice.

Patrick dropped his suitcase with a thud and reached for the edge of the blanket, not entirely sure what he expected to find when he tugged. The soft navy chenille unwound slowly, then fell to the deck. To his shock and amazement, Alice· was wearing only a lacy red bra and matching bikini panties. He was pretty sure his heart stopped.

"Sweet heaven, what did I do to deserve this?"

"You came back," she said simply. "I hope you don't mind my making myself at home to wait for you."

"Uh, no," he said in a choked voice as he tried to cling to one last shred of sanity. "Alice, I thought we were going to be smart about this."

Her smile spread as she reached for the buttons on his shirt. "We are. I bought an absolutely huge box of condoms."

"Woman, what are you trying to do to me?"

"Isn't that obvious?"

He picked the blanket up from the deck and draped it over her shoulders and pulled it closed in front. He couldn't think with all that bare skin tempting him.

"Why are you here, really?"

Her gaze faltered then, and she took a step back.

"I guess I made a mistake. I thought . . ." She couldn't seem to get the words out.

"I know what you thought," he told her gently. "And I do want you. Believe me, I do. You've just caught me off guard. There are a million and one reasons why we shouldn't rush into anything."

"Name one," she challenged.

"This is a small town. You're a kindergarten teacher. There will be talk, and it won't do your career any good."

She tugged the blanket more tightly around her. "Thank you for your consideration," she said stiffly.

Patrick cupped her chin in his hand and forced her to meet his gaze. "I *am* thinking of you, you know."

Her gaze fell and then she sighed. "I know. I thought if I just showed up here like this, maybe you wouldn't think quite so hard."

He tipped her face up again and lost himself in those golden eyes now sparkling with unshed tears. "Don't you dare cry," he whispered, his voice husky.

"I'm not going to cry," she retorted.

"Good, because it would kill me to think that I'd hurt you, especially when I'm trying so damn hard to do the right thing."

"To hell with the right thing," she said fiercely.

Patrick barely contained a smile. "How about I make some coffee and we discuss that, darlin', because you are all about doing the right thing."

"Not always," she muttered, but she trailed him into the boat's cabin, grabbed up her clothes and went into the small head to change.

Patrick started the coffee and waited a very long time for her to emerge. "You ever going to come out?" he finally called out.

"No."

He laughed. "The coffee's ready. And I found an apple pie sitting on my counter. It looks delicious. I have some ice cream in the freezer I could put on top."

The door to the bathroom opened, and Alice emerged, her cheeks flushed and her eyes still just a little too bright.

"Sit," he said, putting a cup of coffee in front of her along with a slice of pie with ice cream.

He sat down across from her and took a long sip of coffee, watching her over the rim of the cup.

"I'm sorry," she said eventually.

"Don't you dare be sorry. You have nothing to apologize for," he said. "Any man would welcome what you tried to do tonight. I'm just trying to be sensible."

"Sometimes sensible sucks."

He laughed. "Tell me about it."

She regarded him with a wistful expression. "After you called last night, I couldn't get you out of my head. It's been a long time since any man made me feel the way you do. It's been an even longer time since I followed an impulse like the one that brought me over here to wait for you."

"I'm glad you followed this one," he insisted.

"Yeah, I could see that," she said wryly.

"I am," he repeated. "It shows we're on the same wavelength, even if the timing is a little off."

She studied him intently. "Okay, you're going to have to explain that one. What's wrong with the timing?"

"Can you honestly tell me that you're ready to get involved with a man who has as many issues with his family as I do?"

"I wasn't here to propose," she said with an edge of sarcasm.

"I'm aware of that, but a proposition is just as dangerous under the circumstances," he said. "I'm comfortable with the way things are with my family. For your own very valid reasons, you disagree. That's going to be a problem between us, especially if you think you're going to get me to change."

"But—"

"Let me finish," he said, cutting her off. "I know why you feel the way you do. I understand that you have regrets about not reconciling with your own family. I respect your feelings, but our situations are entirely different."

"They're not that different," Alice insisted. She leaned forward and added, "I'm not asking you to move back home. I just want you to open the lines of communication."

Patrick frowned at her. "And that's exactly what I mean about the timing being all wrong for us. I can't be with someone who doesn't respect my decision to cut all ties with my family. God knows, I wish that weren't sitting squarely between us, but it is. You'll be on my case nonstop and you know it. Next thing you know we'll be fighting all the time. What's the point?"

"You're just being stubborn," she accused. "About your family and about this."

"Maybe so."

She seemed startled that he didn't deny it. "Then you can change."

"I don't want to change."

"Patrick—"

He looked directly into her eyes. "Leave it alone, Alice, or we won't have anything to discuss at all."

She started to push back from the table and stand up, then sat back down and regarded him with a steady look. "Where did you see this thing between us going?"

"There's a part of me—a huge part of me—that wants exactly what you wanted when you came here tonight. I've spent a lot of hours this past week dreaming about taking you to bed." He sighed heavily. "Then my brain kicks in and I see how wrong that would be, because I can't give you what you really want from me."

Her gaze narrowed. "What do you think I want from you?"

He held her gaze. "A second chance to make things right with your parents."

She gasped at his words, and this time tears did spill down her cheeks. "You're wrong," she all but shouted at him. "That is so unfair."

"I don't think so. I think you believe if you can settle things between me and my folks, it will make up for the reconciliation you never got to have with your own. It won't, Alice. I can't fix what happened in your life. I can't make the regrets go away."

His heart ached as he watched her shoulders sag with defeat. Whether she admitted it or not, he knew he was right. Her expectations were totally unrealistic. Even if he agreed with her and made peace with his family, it would never be what she really needed. If she was going to find peace, she was going to have to dig deep inside and find a way to forgive herself.

He stood up then and held out his hand. "Come on. I'll drive you home."

"I have my car," she said, angrily brushing away the tears that were still falling.

"I know. I'll take you and walk back. You're in no condition to drive."

"I'm fine. I don't want you to drive me."

"Then I'll walk you home," he said, snatching the keys from the table and stuffing them into his pocket. "You're not getting behind the wheel of a car when you're this upset."

"As if I'd let a stubborn man like you upset me," she returned, but she stood up. "Fine. We'll walk." She scowled up at him. "But I don't want to hear a word out of you. I'm furious with you."

Patrick bit back a grin. "Yes, ma'am," he said dutifully.

"And don't even think about trying to kiss me good-night."

"The thought won't even cross my mind," he assured her.

She sniffed, then blew her nose on the tissue he held out for her.

"Oh, don't look so damn smug," she said.

He tried to wipe all expression from his face. "How's that?"

"Better," she said, a hint of satisfaction in her voice.

They set off for her house, the silence between them thick with tension. Patrick remained true to his word. He kept his mouth firmly clamped shut. Alice kept sneaking little sideways glances in his direction, as if to reassure herself that he wasn't about to launch into some sort of chitchat.

The wind had kicked up, and the temperatures had fallen. Alice was plainly shivering as they climbed the hill to her cottage, but he resisted the temptation to offer his jacket or to put his arm around her. She'd set the rules, and he intended to do his utmost to follow them, even if they were ridiculous.

When they reached her house, he noted the white picket fence with its tumble of climbing rose vines. In a few weeks, the roses would bloom in a profusion of color. He could hear the sound of the surf crashing against the cliff behind the house and the slap of a loose shutter somewhere on the house.

"I'll come by tomorrow and fix that shutter," he said.

"I can fix it myself," she said.

He grinned at her disgruntled tone. "Never said you couldn't. It was meant as a peace offering."

"You can't make peace with a couple of nails," she retorted.

"What will it take, then?"

She stared up at him, her face pale in the moon's glow. Her expression was bleak. "I honestly don't know," she said in a tone filled with regret.

"Alice, I was just trying to be honest earlier. I don't want to hurt you by letting you think that you can change me at some point down the road."

"As much as I hate it, I know that," she said.

Patrick shoved his hands in his pockets to keep from reaching for her. "What happens now?"

"I wish I knew."

"What do you want to happen?"

"I suppose you're going to continue to insist that

170

there shouldn't be a difference between what I want right this second and what I want in the global scheme of things," she said wistfully.

"Probably, but try me," he said, fighting a grin.

"Right this second I want you to kiss me," she whispered, her gaze locked with his.

Patrick's heart slammed against his ribs. The woman was tormenting him. "And over the long haul?"

"A lot more kisses," she said, her expression hopeful.

"Alice," he chided.

"I want everyone to live happily ever after," she said.

"With my family," he guessed, finishing the thought.

She sighed. "Yes. So, sue me."

"No," he said. "But I think I will kiss you, if you don't mind. All this talk about kissing has made me just a little wild and crazy."

A smile tugged at her lips. "Oh, really?"

"Yes, really," he said. "As if you didn't know." Hands still shoved determinedly into his pockets so he wouldn't reach for her, he lowered his head and touched his lips to hers. His pulse bucked. "Oh, to hell with it," he murmured, dragging her to him and turning the kiss into something dark and dangerous and intoxicating.

He was aware of her soft gasp of surprise, of her body melting into his. The salt air left their skin damp and whipped her hair so that silky strands brushed over his skin like the tantalizing flick of a feather. He tangled his fingers in all those dark, silky threads of hair and savored the heat where his mouth held hers captive. Fire licked through his veins. The sweet taste of cinnamon and sugar and apple lingered on her tongue.

He wanted more. He wanted too much. And none of his thoroughly rational arguments seemed to matter.

"Come inside," she whispered. "Make love to me, Patrick. It doesn't have to be about tomorrow, or next week. It just has to be about tonight."

He was tempted. Oh, how he was tempted! His body was all but commanding him to take her up on her invitation, but of all the lessons he'd been taught over the years, at least one had stuck. A man didn't take advantage of a woman. And that's what he'd be doing, even if Alice claimed that she could be satisfied with tonight and nothing more.

Besides, buried deep inside was the first tiny kernel of a shocking discovery about himself. He—a man who'd seen the dark side of love and the devastating damage it could do—suddenly wanted to believe in forever.

"Go inside," he said, his hand gentle against her cheek.

Tears welled up in her eyes, along with a familiar flash of anger. "I won't ask again," she said.

"I know that," he said, filled with regret.

Maybe, if things ever changed—whether her expectations or his—he would be the one to ask. And if there was a God in heaven, Alice would forgive him for tonight and say yes.

Chapter Ten

Alice pretty much wanted to die of embarrassment. Twice she'd thrown herself at Patrick, and twice he'd rejected her. Oh, he'd said all sorts of noble things, but the bottom line was he'd been able to say no to everything she was offering. Which meant what? That he was a saint and she was a slut? Now there was a combination destined for happily ever after, she thought bitterly. She'd finally taken her heart out of cold storage and this was what she got for it.

Of course, maybe she'd again leaped too soon. Wasn't that a bitter lesson she should have learned long ago?

She stood under the shower for what seemed like an eternity, but she didn't feel one bit better when she emerged. Maybe that was because not even that much water could wash away all the salt from her self-deprecating tears. She was such an idiot.

She stepped into her bedroom, wrapped in a towel, just in time to hear the phone ring. She glared at it and almost didn't answer, but the ingrained habit of never ignoring phone calls prevented her from letting it ring more than three times.

"Hello." There was no mistaking the testiness in her voice.

"You sound cheery," Molly said. "Anything wrong?"

"Not a thing," Alice said, deliberately forcing a happier note into her voice if only to avoid all the questions likely to be on the tip of Molly's tongue. "Why are you calling so late?"

"Because your car's sitting in my parking lot, and Patrick's sitting at my bar staring into a beer with a moody expression," Molly said, her tone wry. "I figured there's a story there."

"Ask him."

"I did. He told me to mind my own business."

"Well, there you go. Sounds like good advice to me," Alice said.

"You're not going to tell me what's going on?" Molly asked.

"Nope."

"Then I'll have to draw my own conclusions," she said. "A lover's spat, that's what I think. Whose fault was it?"

"No spat. No fault." It wasn't entirely a lie. She and Patrick hadn't exactly fought over his stubborn refusal to have sex with her. He'd taken a stance and she'd had little choice but to accept his decision.

"Yeah, right," Molly said, her voice filled with skepticism. "And I'm Winnie the Pooh."

"Come to think of it, you do bear a remarkable resemblance to him," Alice said. "All round and with that cute little upturned nose of yours."

175

"Not funny," Molly retorted. "Okay, if you're not going to cough up any valuable information, I'll go back and try my luck with Patrick again. He usually caves after a few beers. He's on his second now."

"Leave the man alone," Alice advised, almost feeling sorry for him. Molly could be more relentless than a nor'easter when she put her mind to it.

"Because you don't want me to upset him, or because you're afraid he'll talk?"

"He won't talk," Alice said with confidence. What man would willingly admit he'd turned down sex when it was offered? Besides, if he was noble enough to say no, he was certainly too noble to kiss and tell.

"We'll see," Molly taunted. "And by the way, if I find out you did anything to hurt him, I'll be over there to tear your hair out."

Alice sighed. "He's very lucky to have you as a friend. You know that, don't you?"

"I like to think so," Molly said. "And it works both ways. Patrick's been a rock for me, too."

"When did you need someone to lean on, Molly?" Alice asked, overcome with curiosity. Molly had never seemed the type to need anyone to bolster her spirits or to drag her back from the edge of despair. Once more Alice had the feeling that it had something to do with Daniel Devaney.

"Everyone needs a friend," Molly replied lightly. "You should remember that."

"I know it all too well," Alice insisted.

"Okay, then. Stop by after school tomorrow. I'm making meat loaf and mashed potatoes for the special."

"I'll be there as long as they're not being served with a lot of personal questions thrown in for dessert."

"Can't promise that," Molly said. "Be here anyway."

"I may have things to do," Alice hedged. Scrubbing the toilet was an option. The bathroom could always use another thorough cleaning.

"Be here," Molly repeated, then hung up before Alice could argue.

Alice sighed. Once her friend got a notion in her head, there would be no peace until she had the answers she wanted. Alice figured she'd be up all night trying to come up with some that would satisfy Molly and not make herself look like a complete idiot in the process.

Patrick knew that Molly wasn't going to rest until she figured out what had gone on between him and Alice. She'd pestered him for an hour the night before until he'd finally left the bar just to get some peace and quiet. He also knew she was going to pull the same stunt with Alice. He doubted Alice would be up to fending off Molly, especially if Molly made it seem that she knew more than she did. She was tricky that way. She'd almost gotten to him by hanging up the phone and claiming that Alice had already told her side of the story. He'd realized differently at the last second and kept his own mouth clamped firmly shut. Alice might not be so quick to catch on.

He told himself that was why he was waiting outside the school when the bell rang at the end of the first day back from their late spring break. Kids streamed from the building, their shouts filling the air as they raced to meet waiting moms or to climb onto school buses. Ricky Foster spotted Patrick and came charging straight at him, hitting him with a tackle that would have felled a lot of people. Patrick merely absorbed the shock of contact and steadied the excited boy, thinking about the day when that energy and raw expertise could be put to the football team's advantage.

"Hey, Patrick, how you doing?" Ricky asked, as if they were longtime buddies.

Patrick grinned. "I'm doing okay, Ricky. How was your first day back at school?"

"Awesome. Miss Newberry bought us a hamster. We're going to take care of it."

Patrick couldn't hide his surprise. "School will be out in a few weeks. Who's going to take care of it this summer?"

Ricky shrugged. "She is, I guess. She said something about it reminding her of some rat or something. I didn't get it."

Unfortunately, Patrick did. Apparently the

woman had bought the class a hamster to have a symbolic reminder of him right under her nose. That didn't bode well for the way the afternoon was likely to go.

"Does this hamster have a name?" he inquired uneasily.

"Miss Newberry let us choose. We're calling him Rocky. We figure he needs a tough name, 'cause he's kinda cute."

Patrick chuckled. "Rocky. That's a good one."

Ricky leaned close. "I thought I heard Miss Newberry call him something else, though, something not very nice."

"Did she indeed?"

Patrick looked up just in time to see Alice emerging from the building. The brisk wind plastered her dress to her curves and whipped the skirt above her knees. He went hard just staring at her. That was a very bad sign. He'd hoped they could get off to a fresh start today without their hormones getting in the way.

Patrick felt a tug on his sleeve and looked down into Ricky's upturned face.

"I gotta go," Ricky announced. "Can I come see your boat sometime?"

"If your dad brings you," Patrick told him.

"All right!" Ricky enthused. "I'll tell him tonight."

He rushed off, tripping over his own feet twice on the way to the school bus. Patrick grinned. The kid was exactly like his dad. He couldn't help wondering what that would be like, having a pint-size version of yourself around.

"You shouldn't get so much enjoyment out of another person's pain," Alice said as she came closer.

"How can you not smile at a kid who's that full of energy and zest for life?" he countered. "Nothing keeps him down, not falling in the freezing ocean or falling on his face."

Her expression softened. "I know what you mean. Ricky's one of a kind."

He looked her in the eye. "So, Alice, do you bounce back, too?"

She regarded him warily. "That depends."

"On?"

"Whether I fall down or get shoved."

He sighed heavily. "I didn't shove you."

"That's what it felt like. Maybe you've never experienced rejection twice in one night. Trust me, it sucks."

"I had good reasons," he said, instantly on the defensive.

"So you think."

"Alice, be reasonable."

"Pardon me if I'm not feeling very reasonable at the moment."

"I gathered that." He met her gaze. "I heard about the substitute rat."

A smile tugged at the corners of her mouth. "Symbolic, don't you think?"

"You planning on cutting off any important parts to make a point?" he inquired.

"An interesting thought, but no. I'm not quite that bloodthirsty. Why are you here, by the way? Were you hoping to turn me down yet again?"

He scowled at her. "No."

"What, then? Are you thinking of enrolling in elementary school? I think you're a little too big for the chairs."

"Can it, Alice," he said, not even trying to contain his irritation at her attitude. "We need to talk about Molly. She has questions."

Alice sighed then. "Tell me about it. She called last night. When I wouldn't tell her anything, she said she was going to cross-examine you. Did you tell her anything?"

"No."

"Okay, then. There's no problem. We don't even have to try to keep our stories straight."

"If you think Molly's going to accept our evasions, you don't know her very well. She won't let up until one of us cracks."

"It won't be me," Alice assured him.

"Did she talk you into coming in this afternoon for meat loaf?" he asked.

Her gaze narrowed. "Yes. You, too?"

"Yes. I rest my case."

"I see your point," she conceded with obvious reluctance.

"Maybe we should stick together," he suggested.

She gave him a look that told him just what she thought of his idea.

"Why don't I go by Jess's and deal with Molly and you stay away?" she retorted.

"Because meat loaf and mashed potatoes are my favorites," he said, not about to be banished from the bar because he and Alice couldn't see eye to eye about sex.

"Get them to go," Alice advised. "Once you've left, I'll go in."

His annoyance with her attitude deepened. "Forget it. I prefer to eat right there where things are hot from the oven," he said. "Of course, you can always take your dinner home if you're scared to be around me."

She frowned at that. "I'm not scared of you, Devaney. I'm not scared of anything."

He actually believed that. "Then have dinner with me."

"Why? What's the point?"

He grinned at her testy tone. "Don't tell me you're one of those unenlightened women who believes that men and women can't be friends."

"Of course not. I just believe it's impossible for you and me to be friends."

"Why?"

"It just is, okay?"

"The sex thing, I suppose."

"Don't try and dismiss it. It's not as if it's a simple matter of you hating green beans and me loving them. Sex requires two people to be on the same wavelength."

"Then again, not having sex only requires one person to take a stance for all the right reasons," he said. "I never said I didn't want you in my life."

"On your terms."

"Yes, on my terms, because I'm trying to be sensible. You're not."

"How lovely that you think so highly of me. Since we obviously want different things from this relationship, it's better to cut our losses."

He leveled a look straight into her eyes. "So that's it? Sex is all you want from me?"

She frowned at him. The pulse at the base of her throat was beating rapidly. "I didn't say that."

"Didn't you? That's what I heard. If we can't sleep together, then you don't want anything from me. Correct me if I've got that wrong."

She looked as if she wanted to smack him, but she was far too ladylike to do it. "I'm just saying that the whole sex thing will get in the way of anything else."

"Speak for yourself. I learned to control myself a long time ago. I don't have to jump into bed with a woman just because she gets to me."

"Dammit, Patrick, this is getting us nowhere."

"No, I think it is. I think it's very telling that you don't think you're capable of keeping your raging hormones under control around me."

"Don't you dare twist this around and make it my problem," she said furiously.

"Then whose problem is it? I'm willing to be friends, to get to know you better. You're the one who won't settle for anything less than a passionate relationship, right here and right now."

"So, you're saying this is a matter of timing, that one day you might change your mind?"

Not if he had a brain in his head, but yeah, sooner or later, she was going to get to him. Better not to tell her that, though. "Maybe," he equivocated.

"Just what I love, a man who knows how to make a firm commitment." She glared at him. "Okay, then. You want a friend, I'll be your friend," she said through gritted teeth. "But I've got to tell you, right this second I don't like you very much."

He bit back a grin and reached for her hand. "Come on, friend. Let's have dinner."

She jerked her hand away. "Don't touch me."

He did laugh then. "*Too* friendly?"

"Too presumptuous," she shot back.

As they strolled toward Jess's he glanced sideways at her. "You know, if we walk into the bar barely speaking to each other, Molly's going to be all over us."

"Don't kid yourself. She's going to be all over us no matter what we do," Alice retorted. "At least this way, we're being honest about how we feel."

"Are we?"

She stopped and whirled on him. "What do you want from me? I'm doing the best I can to find some middle ground we can both live with. You think sex is too complicated with us, that's your right, but don't accuse me of being dishonest about my feelings."

He nodded slowly. "That's fair. You're right. There's bound to be a certain amount of pretense while we're working this out."

"Do you even know how to be friends with a woman?"

"Sure. Molly and I have been friends for years."

"And the thought of jumping into the sack with her never once crossed your mind?"

"Never once," he said honestly. Molly had always had her eye on another Devaney. And even now, after things had gone terribly wrong between her and Daniel, she wouldn't look at another man, much less at Daniel's twin brother. Patrick had always respected that.

"Well, good for you. Maybe you are a saint, after all."

"Not a saint," he insisted. "I'm just trying to be an honorable man and not take advantage of the situation."

"Oh, whatever," she said. "From now on you're not going to have to worry about taking advantage of the 'situation,' as you put it. I wouldn't sleep with you if you were the last man on earth."

He met her gaze. "Is that so?"

She swallowed hard but didn't blink or look away. "Yes, that's so."

He nodded slowly. "Good. Then we have nothing to worry about."

Except for the fact that right that second he wanted nothing more than to sweep her into his arms and make love to her for about forty-eight hours, nonstop.

Pride was the only thing that made Alice walk into Jess's with Patrick by her side. It was also the only thing that had kept her from swinging her very hefty tote bag and smacking him upside the head when he got that smug expression on his face. It was going to be a long evening. She should have sacrificed the meat loaf and gone home to one of the frozen dinners she kept in the freezer for emergencies. Then again, that would have been admitting to Patrick that she couldn't spend a few hours in his company without getting all hot and bothered.

The minute they entered the bar, Molly gave the two of them a thorough once-over, then nodded in satisfaction. "Pick a booth. I'll bring you a couple of beers and the special in a sec," she said as she took a tray of icy mugs of ale to a table of fishermen seated in the middle of the room. She deftly managed to set the drinks on the table, all the while avoiding a few friendly, roving hands.

Molly rarely lost her cool, Alice thought with admiration. She could keep an entire room filled with rowdy men under control with just one withering glance. Alice wondered if she ought to take lessons from her. Maybe if she perfected her own withering glance, Patrick would stop tormenting her with all this nonsense about friendship. The odds of them sharing a purely platonic friendship were somewhere between slim and none. In her experience, once chemistry had been unleashed, it was all but impossible to pretend it didn't exist.

Still, since he'd insisted on the ground rules, she wasn't about to suggest that she couldn't follow them. She'd just have to train herself to pretend he was as attractive as sludge. Sooner or later, maybe she could make herself believe it.

Besides, Patrick was right about one thing: they hardly knew each other. She'd fallen for his heroics when he'd rescued Ricky, for the vulnerability she sensed in him and for the lost soul she imagined him to be. In truth, he seemed pretty darned determined not to be the least bit lost. In fact, he seemed pretty confident about himself and the decisions he'd made. Maybe if she got to know the real Patrick Devaney, she'd discover that without the imagined vulnerabilities, he didn't appeal to her in the slightest.

She clung to the icy mug of beer Molly had brought to the table and peered at Patrick thoughtfully. "Why did you decide to become a fisherman?" she asked.

His gaze narrowed at the question, as if he suspected it were some sort of trap. "I like being on the water," he said eventually. "It's a challenge."

Alice persisted. "Is it something you always wanted to do?"

He shook his head. "No. A long time ago I wanted to be a fireman, and then for a brief period I considered being an engineer on a train."

"How old were you when you changed your mind?"

"Seven."

A chuckle erupted before she could catch it. "What happened?"

"I caught my first big fish. I was standing on shore when it happened. My dad had to help me reel it in. It probably weighed no more than a pound, but I thought it was huge. My mom cooked it for dinner that night. It was the best fish I've ever had. After that, my dad started taking me out on his boat on Saturdays. He taught me everything he knew about commercial fishing." His expression turned sad. "I always thought we'd go into business together once I grew up."

Alice opened her mouth to tell him it wasn't too late, then clamped it shut again. She'd promised not to go there. Besides, he was opening up. She didn't want to do anything to jeopardize this momentary peace between them.

He sighed heavily. "But things change. I got my own boat and went into business for myself. I like the independence."

"Still, it must be exhausting."

"Some days, yes," he conceded. "But I'm my own boss."

"Ever give yourself a day off?"

"All the time."

"What do you do when you're off?"

He grinned at her. "I go fishing."

She stared at him in astonishment. "What?"

"I take a pole and go off to one of the lakes and stand on shore, just the way I did when I was a kid."

"You find that relaxing?"

"Absolutely. It's not the same at all. When I'm out at sea, I have to stay focused every second. Too many things can go wrong in a heartbeat. When I'm at the lake, I can close my eyes, feel the sun on my face, let my thoughts wander and wait for the fish to bite. If they do, great. If they don't, I've still spent the day outdoors in a great setting."

"It sounds tranquil," she said wistfully.

"It is. Play your cards right and I'll take you sometime."

Alice almost jumped on his reference to cards and that losing night of poker he'd had, then restrained herself. She saw that he was watching her expectantly, clearly anticipating that she'd remind him of their bet. All the more reason to avoid the subject.

"What kind of music do you like?" she asked instead.

He seemed startled by the change of topic, but went along with it. "Country-western, mostly. It gets at the heart of things."

"Movies?"

"Never go."

"Books?"

"Tom Clancy, John Grisham."

"Guy books," she scoffed.

"Hey, I *am* a guy. What do you want from me? Were you hoping I had a secret addiction to romance novels?"

She grinned at that. "You might learn something."

His lips curved into an irrepressible smile. "I might at that. You have any around the house I could borrow?"

"Buy your own."

"Maybe I will. Then, when I'm properly in touch with my feelings, we can have this conversation again." He gave her a long look. "Exactly what is this conversation we're having, anyway?"

"It's called friendly conversation," she said. "It's what you said you wanted."

He nodded slowly, as if trying to grasp the concept. "Okay, then, my turn. Why did you become a teacher?"

"I love kids, especially at the kindergarten age.

They still have this incredible curiosity, and they can sop up knowledge like a sponge."

"They're also a little rambunctious," he pointed out.

"I love that, too. It keeps it challenging. I have to be on my toes to keep their attention."

"You want kids of your own?"

"Sure."

"How many?"

"Three, maybe four."

"Really? Then shouldn't you be getting started?"

She frowned. It was a sore point. She wasn't really old at twenty-six, but unless she wanted to have back-to-back babies, the clock was going to start ticking soon. "I'm not that old," she told him.

He grinned. "Older than me. I could have babies for, say, the next forty years or so."

"Typical of a man," she chided. "You think just because your parts work longer than ours, you'd make good daddy material."

"Okay, a valid point," he said, just as Molly appeared at the table, her expression thoroughly fascinated.

"Discussing having a family?" she inquired. "How interesting."

"Don't make too much out of it," Alice said. "We were talking in generalities." She barely resisted the urge to explain that it was all but impossible to have a child with a man who wouldn't agree to

191

sleep with her. That was a can of worms best left tightly shut.

"Still, it's a start," Molly said cheerfully, settling into the booth next to Alice. "I've never heard Patrick mention a need to have children before."

"I said I could," he retorted. "Not that I intended to."

Alice stared at him. "You don't want children?"

"I didn't say that, either," he replied defensively.

"What then?"

"Just that I didn't have much of an example in the father department, as it turns out. I'm not sure I want to risk blowing things as badly as he did."

"That's absurd," Molly and Alice said together.

"You'd make a terrific father," Alice added. "Look at the way you were with Ricky the other day."

"And look at how the kids adore it when you coach Little League," Molly added. She turned to Alice. "You should see him. He's like the Pied Piper, with a dozen adoring kids trailing after him."

"I can imagine," Alice said, liking the image that crept into her head and wouldn't leave. "Are you coaching this summer?"

He shrugged. "Probably."

"I'll have to come to the games. I love baseball."

For the first time since she'd started poking around to discover his likes and dislikes, his eyes lit up. "You do?"

"I spent a lot of evenings at the Red Sox games when I lived in Boston. In a weird way, it made me feel close to my dad. He was a huge fan."

"Little League in Widow's Cove isn't quite the same as the Red Sox," Patrick pointed out.

"But where do you think I saw my first baseball games?" she said, suddenly filled with nostalgia. "My dad never went to Boston, but he did take me over to the ballfields here every Saturday afternoon. A lot of my friends were on teams. Then at night we'd listen to the Red Sox games on the radio."

"I did the same thing with my dad," he said, though his expression remained shuttered.

Alice instinctively reached out and covered his hand with her own. Funny thing how their relationships with their dads had brought them together yet again, this time over a shared interest in baseball. It was such a small thing, she thought, but maybe it was something they could build on.

Chapter Eleven

Alice glanced out her classroom window just after lunchtime the next day and saw storm clouds building. It had been unseasonably hot and humid, and clearly they were about to pay for it. Normally there was nothing she liked better than a good, cleansing storm, but a sudden image of Patrick caught out at sea made her insides clench.

Come on, she told herself. He knows what he's doing. By his own admission, Patrick had been around boats all his life. Surely he knew enough to come into port with a storm on the horizon. Surely he knew to find a safe harbor.

But what if there hadn't been time? The thought hit her just as lightning streaked from the sky and thunder rumbled. Her already restless students reacted with alarm. Abandoning her lesson plan for the afternoon, Alice chose a favorite story about the Rainbow Fish and called the class to the front of the room.

Francesca crowded close to her side and even the usually independent Ricky pulled his chair closer than usual. She gave them all a reassuring smile, then tried not to ruin the effect by jumping at another bolt of lightning that seemed to hit far too close for comfort.

"Okay, now," she said, keeping her tone

soothing. "Anybody remember what this story is about?"

"Sharing," Francesca said in her shy little voice, leaning against Alice.

"Exactly." Alice opened the book and began to read about the lonely fish with the glittering scales that set him apart from all the other fish.

Normally the story had the power to captivate her, but today just the mention of fish sent her thoughts ricocheting right back to Patrick. Still, the students' excited questions and rapt attention provided a distraction that lasted until the bell rang.

Alice noted the rain lashing at the windows in sheets and realized the kids were going to get soaked just getting to the buses and to their parents' cars. Since the day had started with bright sunshine, none of them had rain gear with them.

Grabbing her own umbrella from the coat closet, she herded her class into a line and led them to the front door, where several of the moms were already waiting. When those students were on their way, Alice put up her umbrella and took the rest one by one to their buses. The umbrella was virtually useless in the whipping wind, but it was the best she could do. She sighed when the last of her charges were finally safely aboard their buses or with their moms.

Her gaze instantly went toward the waterfront, but it was too far away for her to realistically hope to catch a glimpse of Patrick's boat. She was debating running across the park to get a better look when the principal appeared at her side.

"It's a nasty afternoon, isn't it?" Loretta said to Alice. "I understand several of the local fishermen were caught at sea."

Alice's heart began to pound. "Have you heard which ones?"

The principal gave her a knowing look. "I imagine it's Patrick Devaney you're most concerned about."

Alice didn't waste her breath trying to deny it. "Is he back?"

"No," Loretta admitted, "but I'm sure he's fine. Patrick's a smart man. Fishing and the sea are in his blood. He knows what to do to remain safe."

Alice nodded, but she wasn't nearly as certain as the principal seemed to be. Oh, she believed he was highly skilled, but she doubted that any man was a match for Mother Nature when she decided to stir the elements into a frenzy of wind and rain.

Loretta gave her a sympathetic look. "I've canceled the teachers' meeting, if you'd like to go down to the docks and check on him. Perhaps by the time you get there, someone will have more news."

Alice gave her a grateful look, went inside to grab her purse, then took off running, oblivious to the rain that soaked her dress and washed away the little makeup she wore. When she reached the dock with its useless No Trespassing sign, she skidded to a halt and stared out at the churning gray waters as far as she could see through the thick haze. If Patrick was heading for port, she couldn't spot him.

She shivered as the temperature dropped, then wrapped her arms around herself in a useless attempt to keep warm. With the afternoon heat bumping straight into the cold air from the northwest, there would be fog soon. Getting back to port then would be an even trickier task, notwithstanding all the latest navigational equipment.

Getting colder by the minute, Alice found a blue tarp weighted down with an old anchor and dragged it free, then huddled beneath its scant protection.

That was how Molly found her hours later as darkness fell and more and more people gathered along the shore to watch for the handful of still-missing boats.

"I can't believe you're out here with no coat or hat," Molly scolded. "When someone told me they'd seen you, I was sure they'd been wrong. I thought you had more sense."

"Patrick's not back yet," Alice explained. "I couldn't leave."

Molly gave her a commiserating look. "You've got it bad, don't you?"

Alice sighed. "I suppose I do, for all the good it's going to do me." She shook her head. "I can't think about that now." She gazed at Molly worriedly. "Do you think Patrick's okay?"

"I think he's probably out there leading the rescue attempts for any of the other boats that are in trouble, that's what I think," Molly said with conviction.

"Really?" Alice asked, searching her friend's face.

"Absolutely."

There wasn't so much as a hint of doubt in Molly's voice, but Alice still wasn't entirely comforted. "I hope you're right," she whispered, trying to see through the gathering darkness for any sign of an approaching boat. He had to come back, if only so she could tell him that she would be his friend and ask nothing more, if that's the way it had to be. All that mattered was that Patrick be safe.

Patrick was cursing himself every which way as his boat rocked and rolled on the huge swells and lightning split the sky again and again. Normally he had a nose for bad weather and he could smell an oncoming storm in the air.

Today, though, his mind had been on Alice, on their dads and baseball and on the uneasy truce they'd reached the night before. He'd missed all the signs that the weather was about to change dramatically.

By the time he'd noticed the first dark clouds on

the horizon, it had been too late. The storm was on top of him in minutes, with its fierce winds and pelting rain. The deck turned slippery and treacherous, and waves washed over the sides of the trawler.

"Blast it all to hell and back," he muttered as he tried to keep his hands steady on the wheel. He'd never gotten caught like this before. In fact, he was usually among the first to get back to shore and the first to head back out when a storm died down to look for others who hadn't been as lucky.

Today it was going to require every ounce of his concentration to keep from making a mistake that could mean certain death, either from the boat capsizing or him being washed overboard because of some misstep on the slippery deck. He thought of Alice and concluded he'd have to make damn sure nothing like that happened. He had fences to mend with the woman. He had to tell her that she was right and he was wrong. They needed to grab every second they could to be together, because life was filled with uncertainties.

Maybe their relationship would last, maybe it was doomed, but the only way to find out was to take a chance. He intended to say all that and to eat all the crow she wanted to dish up. Then he intended to make love to her for hours on end until he'd finally had his fill of touching and exploring and making her cry out with pleasure.

Hands clenched tightly to the wheel, he heard the

sputtering static of his radio and a frantic Mayday call from another Widow's Cove boat. He peered around through the almost impenetrable wall of rain for some sign of a boat nearby.

"Where are you, *Lady Q.?*" he radioed back. "Give me your location."

He heard the hint of panic in Ray Stover's voice as he responded with the coordinants. Ray was a practiced seaman. If he was showing any hint of fear, then the danger had to be high.

"We're taking on water fast, Patrick. Are you anywhere close?"

"Close enough," Patrick said, trying to hide his concern. "Not to worry. I'll get to you, Ray. Hang in there. Got your life vest on?"

"Of course."

"If anything happens to the boat, get the light on and keep signaling. I'll be there any minute now."

Totally focused on the emergency task, he set the boat's course and calculated that he could be there in ten minutes, maybe fifteen if the sea fought him, which it seemed inclined to do. Grabbing a spotlight he kept for emergencies, he sent its piercing beam in the direction where the sinking boat would likely appear.

"Ray, I've got a spotlight shining. Let me know when you see it."

"Roger that," Ray said, the tension in his voice less palpable. "Which direction?"

"I'm just east of you and approaching from the south."

"Got it."

The rain was finally easing and the lightning had moved farther out to sea, but the swells were still a challenge as Patrick cut through the water toward the distressed boat.

His radio crackled.

"I see the light," Ray shouted triumphantly. "You're about a hundred yards away now, and just in the nick of time, buddy. This crate of mine is about to go down."

Patrick still didn't breathe a sigh of relief, not until he was alongside the rapidly sinking *Lady Q.*, which was listing to port with water washing over its bow. As soon as he pulled alongside and held out a hand, Ray gingerly made the leap onto the deck of the *Katie G.* His lined face was stoic until the weathered and once-sturdy boat sank from view, then his expression filled with sorrow.

"Hey, man, you're okay. That's what counts," Patrick consoled him. "You can always get another boat."

Ray shook his head. "I'm done," he said, his voice heavy with resignation. "I've had three close calls in the past two years. I want to live to see my grandchildren grow up. Janey's been nagging at me to retire, but I figured I'd do one more season before calling it quits. This just pushes things along a little faster."

201

Patrick heard the regret in Ray's voice and knew he'd feel the same when the day finally came that the sea's challenges became too much for him, too. Before he could stop himself, his thoughts wandered to his father, who was almost the same age as Ray. Had he weathered today's storm? The commercial boats he captained were bigger and more seaworthy than the *Katie G.* or the *Lady Q.*, but in a raging storm, few of the boats were truly safe. A line of squalls was something a man learned to respect, if he intended to live a long and healthy life.

Because Patrick didn't want to care about his father's fate today, he busied himself with piloting the boat back toward Widow's Cove and keeping up a steady stream of distracting conversation to keep Ray's mind off of his own near miss.

As the lights of Widow's Cove pierced the darkness of the night sky, Patrick shone his spotlight toward shore to signal that he was coming in. He heard a shout go up.

"Wonder if we lost anyone out there today?" Ray asked. "Damn storm came up quicker than most."

"Yours was the only distress signal I caught," Patrick told him. "I imagine everyone else is making their way back now. If anyone's still missing, we'll know it soon enough."

When Patrick reached the dock, Ray helped him tie up the boat, then reached for Patrick's hand with a strong grip. "I owe you, son."

Patrick gave the old man an embrace. "If you start getting restless being retired, you can go out with me anytime."

Ray grinned. "I might just take you up on that," he said, then cast a guilty glance toward the gray-haired woman standing on the dock with tears streaming down her face. "Assuming Janey ever lets me out of her sight again."

Patrick held back as Ray went to his wife and gently wiped the tears from her cheeks before putting his arm around her and leading her toward Jess's, where the town traditionally gathered in the aftermath of a storm that threatened the lives of the local fishermen.

After they'd gone, Patrick jumped onto the dock, only to walk straight into a shove that caught him off guard and almost landed him on his backside. Seemed like today was destined to be full of unexpected shocks. His gaze narrowed with speculation as he looked into Alice's flashing eyes.

"You scared the living daylights out of me," she said accusingly, her expression filled with a mix of anger and relief. "Don't you ever do that to me again, Patrick Devaney."

He stared at her in disbelief. "You were worried?"

"Look at me," she said, gesturing toward her soaked clothes and dripping hair. "I've been here for hours. I was terrified." Then the tears began rolling down her cheeks, a reaction every bit as heartfelt as Janey Stover's had been.

Shaken by the sight of Alice's tears, Patrick reached for her. "I'm here," he said, drawing her into his arms. "Ah, darlin', don't cry, I'm here now."

She poked him in the chest, though with slightly less force than her earlier shove. "You scared me," she repeated.

He tucked a finger under her chin and looked deep into her eyes. "I can't promise it won't happen again. This is what I do."

She sighed, resting her cheek against his chest. "I know."

He decided to share some of his own discoveries made during the storm. "It did occur to me as I was sitting out there in the dark with the winds howling and the rain coming down that maybe I've been just a little hardheaded about the sex thing," he said casually.

Her gaze shot up to clash with his. "Meaning?"

Patrick felt himself drowning in those golden pools of light, still shimmering with tears. If he hadn't already been certain, one look into her eyes would have convinced him. "I don't want to waste any more time," he said, then added, "that is, if you're still interested."

She stood on tiptoe and kissed him, leaving no doubt at all in his mind about her response. That kiss could have melted steel, he thought, then wondered if maybe it wouldn't be worth weathering a storm every day to have a homecoming like this.

Alice apparently had no intention of giving Patrick one single second to change his mind, he concluded as she gave his chest a gentle nudge.

"Back on the boat," she ordered.

"I think I've had about all the bobbing around on the water I can take for one evening," he countered. "I had in mind a nice, warm bed on dry land."

"If you're considering mine, it's too far away."

"It's a few blocks," he pointed out.

"Too far," she repeated.

"There's always the room above Jess's," he suggested.

She gave him an incredulous look. "Are you crazy? We'd never hear the end of it," Alice said. "Okay, you win. My place, but let's make it snappy."

"I don't suppose I could grab a bite to eat first," he said.

She glowered at him. "If that isn't the most romantic thing I've ever heard. 'Darling, I'd really love to sleep with you after holding out forever, but I'd like my dinner first.'"

"You want me to have a little stamina, don't you?" he teased.

Alice rolled her eyes. "Okay, my place, I feed you and then no more stalling."

Patrick grinned. "No more stalling," he agreed.

As they walked up the hill to her cottage, he took off his jacket and wrapped it around her in an attempt to stop her shivering. As they neared, he spotted the warm light glowing in the front window.

"I thought you hadn't been home," he said. "There's a light on."

"It's on a timer," she explained. "I don't like coming home to a dark house."

Patrick sighed, unable to recall the last time he'd come home to a welcoming light in the window. Most nights his boat was dark as pitch when he got back from Jess's. Until he'd seen the light in Alice's window, he hadn't realized just how depressing the darkness could be.

Walking through the door of her cottage for the first time, he got the oddest sensation in his chest. It felt as if he were coming home. She'd made the place cozy, even on a night like this. The fireplace was ready for the touch of a match. The walls were a soft shade of yellow, the furniture covered in blue-and-white prints and solids. There were fresh flowers in an old cobalt-blue jar on the coffee table next to a pile of books, and a bright-yellow chenille throw had been tossed over the back of the sofa. Patrick could instantly imagine Alice snuggled beneath the yellow fabric, the fire blazing and a book in her hands. He could just as easily imagine her wearing that soft throw and nothing else.

Best not to go there just yet, he admonished himself. To put a little distance between them, he said,

"Why don't you go take a hot shower before you catch pneumonia? I'll see what I can rustle up in the kitchen."

She gave him one of those long, lingering looks that could vaporize water, then said, "Sure you don't want to come take that shower with me?"

Oh, yeah, he thought, feeling a little frantic. That was exactly what he wanted, but if he touched her now, if he so much as caught a glimpse of her naked, they'd be in her bed before either of them could say a word. He didn't want it to happen that way, not the first time they were together. He wanted to give her tenderness and romance and long, slow, tormenting caresses.

"I'll pass," he said mildly.

She gave him a grin that only a practiced vamp could have perfected. "Your loss."

"I'm sure it is," he murmured, turning away to go in search of the kitchen.

Compared to his own, Alice's kitchen was well stocked with homemade soup, the makings for a variety of sandwiches and even a leftover roasted chicken with plenty of meat still on its bones. Patrick's mouth watered as he pulled away a chunk of tender white meat and munched on that while pondering all the other choices.

He put the beef vegetable soup on to heat, then made two thick sandwiches of ham, cheese, lettuce and tomatoes on homemade bread. After pouring two glasses of milk, he set the feast on the kitchen table. He was about to take his first bite, when the faint floral scent of Alice's perfume caught his attention. He glanced up, and his mouth went dry.

She was standing in the kitchen doorway wearing a perfectly respectable robe—that is, if fabric that draped and clung to outline every curve could be described as respectable. It was the same golden-bronze shade as her eyes and it caught the light in much the same way, shimmering provocatively. Suddenly the only thought on his mind was slowly, ever so slowly, stripping that robe off her and letting it slide to the floor.

"Alice, what are you trying to do to me?" he asked, his breath hitching.

She tried to fight a smile, but it escaped, anyway. She fingered the edge of the robe. "What? This old thing?"

"That old thing could drive a man wild."

She seemed genuinely surprised by the vehemence in his voice. "Really?"

"Yes, and you damn well know it," he accused.

Her smile was full-blown now. "I could take it off."

Patrick forgot all about food, forgot everything, including his own name, as his blood turned to fire. "Okay," he murmured, when he could find breath enough to speak.

She blinked once. "Okay?"

He nodded and reached for the loosely tied belt on the robe. "That's what I said, okay. Take it off."

One tug on the belt untied it and had the front of the robe gaping open to reveal a body still glowing from her shower and slightly pink, though he couldn't be certain if the color was due to a thorough scrubbing or embarrassment.

"You take my breath away," he told her with total honesty.

"That's only fair," she said, sliding onto his lap. "You've been stealing mine since the day we met."

"What are we going to do about it?"

She grazed her knuckles along his cheek. "We could start with this," she said, lowering her mouth to cover his.

His pulse ricocheted wildly as he gave himself up to the kiss. She'd clearly intended it to be a light, teasing contact, but it turned greedy and all consuming in a flash. His heart slammed against his ribs, and he bunched a handful of that delicate, silky fabric into a wad to keep from putting his hands all over her.

How could he want her this much? he wondered with a hint of desperation. How had he allowed himself to need anyone this much? Did it even matter?

"Sweetheart, I think a kitchen chair is the wrong place for this," he said, scooping her up as he stood and heading for the door. "Where's the bedroom?"

Her head tucked on his shoulder, her breath fanning against his cheek, she directed him down the hall to her room. The colors in here were as soothing as those in the living room, Patrick noted vaguely as he settled her in the middle of a double bed on which the sheets had already been turned down. She regarded him with a lazy look.

"You're not climbing in here unless you lose some of those clothes, Devaney."

He grinned. "Which ones? Any preference about where I start?"

She studied him thoughtfully. "The shoes and socks first, I think, then the shirt. After that, I'll give it some more thought."

Patrick kicked off his shoes and stripped away his socks, then dragged his flannel shirt over his head without bothering to unbutton more than the top two buttons. "Next?"

"The belt, I think. Slowly, please."

He bit back a grin. "You sure you don't want a little background music for this striptease?"

"Nope. You're doing fine. Now, lose the T-shirt."

"Okay, then," he said, when he was standing before her, bare-chested and surprisingly self-conscious. "There's not a lot left. Do the jeans go or stay for now?"

"They go, of course."

Getting into the spirit of it and enjoying the mischievous pleasure shining in her eyes, he unsnapped the jeans then took his own sweet time unzipping them. He executed a little twirl before sliding them off and kicking them across the room.

Alice laughed. "Nice touch. I like the jockeys, by the way. Red is definitely your color."

"Probably matches my cheeks about now," he said, kneeling on the bed to press a kiss to her lips.

Alice cupped his face in her hands. "You aren't embarrassed, are you?"

"Darlin', what I am is hot and bothered."

Her smile spread. "Well, then, come on over here and let's see what we can do about that."

"I have a few ideas."

"Yes, I imagine you do."

He studied her expression, then chuckled. "But we're doing this your way, am I right?"

She reached for the waistband of his jockeys, her fingers grazing his belly. "Oh, yeah," she said, her eyes bright with anticipation.

"Then, go for it," he said, closing his eyes and lying back against the pillows. "I'm all yours."

He wasn't sure, but he thought he heard her murmur something that sounded a lot like "If only," but then her hands were playing their wicked games, and Patrick completely lost himself in her touch.

Chapter Twelve

Alice had waited too long for Patrick to make love to her to want to rush through it. She intended to torment him until he was at least half as crazy with desire as she'd been for a couple of weeks now.

She sat back on her heels, her robe spilling open to display more bare flesh than she'd exposed to anyone except her doctor in a long time. Patrick was reclining against her pillows, clad in nothing except those bright-red jockey shorts, and she intended to savor the sight. The man was hard as a rock, every muscle well defined, not from working out in a gym but from his daily life. She reached out and ran her fingers over his abdomen and felt the muscles jerk at her touch. She could also see the effect on another well-defined portion of his anatomy, which his jockeys did nothing to disguise.

"Interesting," she murmured, as if she were conducting an experiment.

A low chuckle rumbled in his throat. "Having fun yet?"

"Absolutely," she said, moving on to the warm skin of his broad chest. She tangled her fingers in the shadowing of dark hair that curled tightly against tanned skin. She could feel the heat radiating from him and uttered a little sigh of satisfaction. She hadn't realized how much she missed touching a man like this, how much she missed the closeness with another human being.

Even so, the closeness felt different somehow, more intense. More complete. She realized that because her feelings for Patrick ran deeper, she craved more than physical intimacy with him. She craved the emotional connection that had been building between them.

Not that the physical was all bad. No, indeed, she thought as she leaned forward and pressed a kiss to the base of his throat and felt his pulse leap. Then he clamped his hand on the back of her neck and held her still.

"Enough," he said just before closing his mouth over hers.

His tongue invaded in a heartbeat, stirring sensations low in her belly. Even as his kiss deepened and devastated, his hand was exploring, slipsliding over silky fabric, rubbing it over nipples already taut and sensitive. She was aching and anxious by the time his clever fingers moved lower to dip into moist heat and send her jolting off the mattress.

The man was a wizard, his touch magic. She felt herself convulse from just one delicate flick across the tight bud of her arousal. Waves of pleasure washed over her.

Patrick waited, letting her ride them out, before starting all over again. The buildup was even faster this time, and far more intense. Her already aroused body responded to each caress, to each kiss, with restless movements that quickly turned more frenzied and demanding.

"Not just yet," he said, holding back, his gaze locked with hers.

"I need you now," she insisted, thinking she might die of anticipation if he insisted on waiting another moment. She lifted her hips, seeking the joining he was denying her. "Patrick, please. Inside me."

He smoothed a hand over her brow as if soothing an anxious child. "When the time is right."

Alice bit back a gasp as he swirled his tongue around one nipple, then another, before tugging hard and sending sensation slamming through her. Her hips lifted off the bed, once more seeking relief, seeking him . . . but still he remained beyond reach.

Those clever fingers tormented and teased and inflamed until she thought she'd scream from the sheer wonder of it. Every muscle in her body strained for release, every inch of her skin was hot and aching for a touch that he now passed out with stingy deliberation. Her nerves were raw, her body achy and needy, when at last he thrust into her and took her breath away.

She felt her body stretch, then mold to his, felt the friction as he moved inside her and then the quick rise of sensation, the overwhelming tide of pleasure as heat and desire exploded. Rather than shattering them into a million fragments, the explosion melded them into one single unit, like the fusion of metals into something so strong, so powerful it could withstand the test of time.

Alice clung to Patrick's shoulders and rode out the waves of sensation until, at last, peace followed. And with peace came the certainty that this love she felt for Patrick Devaney would last a lifetime.

If only he would let it.

Morning came too darn soon. Patrick would have stayed right here, Alice warm and flushed in his arms, if there hadn't been the outside world and all its demands to consider. He might be master of his own fate, but she wasn't. She had a classroom full of five-year-olds who were counting on her. He glanced at the clock, noted it was only six and concluded they had at least a little time before Alice would need to start on her workday.

He brushed a finger lightly across her lush lips, then felt the soft whisper of a sigh as she snuggled against him. "Hey, darlin', if you wake up now like a good girl, there's time to be bad before the day gets underway."

"Bad?" she murmured. Then her eyes snapped open, alight with interest. "How bad?"

He grinned at her instantaneous eagerness. That

was just one of things he'd come to love about her during the long night. Alice held nothing back. There was no pretense of reticence, no game playing. When it came to making love, they were completely, shatteringly attuned.

He leaned close to whisper in her ear, the taunt designed to make her cheeks flame and her hands rove. She slid on top of him in a heartbeat, taking him into her and riding him, her head thrown back, her expression triumphant, as another climax tore through them both.

She collapsed on top of him, her breath coming in gasps. "There's a very good chance I won't be able to move for the rest of my life," she murmured eventually.

Patrick grinned. There was far more satisfaction than dismay in her tone. "I think you'd better," he advised lightly. "I'm not sure you want to try explaining away an absence from school today."

She groaned and rolled over. "You could call in for me."

"And say what?" he teased. "That you spent the night making mad, passionate love with me and can't even crawl out of bed?"

"It would be the truth," she said, her eyes still closed, a smile on her lips.

"And it would be all over town by suppertime. It just might give some parents second thoughts about entrusting their precious kindergarten students to you."

She opened her eyes and frowned. "Yeah, I see your point," she conceded with obvious reluctance. "What about you? Are you going to work today? Or are you going to laze around in my bed all day? Come to think of it, I rather like the idea of daydreaming about that all day long. I'd be highly motivated to get home after school."

"Unfortunately, I, too, have to work," he said. "I need to go over the boat to see if there was any damage from the storm. Then I'll probably take it out for a few hours."

Alarm flashed in her eyes for just an instant. "Are you sure? Have you checked the weather?"

"Not yet." He smoothed away the furrow in her brow. "Alice, yesterday was a fluke. I was distracted. I missed all the signs that a storm was approaching. Usually I'm one of the first ones in."

"What happened yesterday?"

"You were on my mind," he admitted.

The furrows instantly formed again. "It was my fault you almost got yourself killed?"

"No. It was mine. I know better than to allow myself to get distracted. It won't happen again." He gave her a nudge. "Now scoot. I'm not sure I can drag myself out of this bed as long as you're in here tempting me."

"I tempt you?" she asked.

"Don't fish for compliments," he scolded. "You know you drive me crazy. There are a million and one reasons why you and me being together is a bad idea, and you managed to make me forget every one of them."

She grinned then. "Good, because you drive me crazy, too."

He watched her finally slide from the bed, then head for the bathroom, unable to tear his gaze away from her amazing body. No question about it, she'd bewitched him.

Unfortunately, there was also no question that their relationship remained every bit as complicated as it had been before they'd slept together. There were some things that making love—or even falling in love—simply couldn't change.

Alice felt as if everything in her life was changing and, finally, for the better. She'd spent her whole life dreaming about a man like Patrick Devaney— solid and dependable and amazingly tender, a man in whom to place her trust, whom she could love with her whole heart, with whom she could build a family. Maybe, at long last, she would be able to fill the hole in her heart that had been left when her own family had died.

"You're certainly glowing this morning," Loretta Dowd said when she came across Alice in the school office. "Obviously, you found Patrick last night. He made it home safely?"

Alice prayed she wasn't blushing furiously, though her cheeks felt hot under the woman's knowing gaze. "He's fine," she said. "He rescued Ray Stover. Ray's boat capsized."

"Janey will be glad enough of that, I imagine," the principal said. "She's been wanting Ray to retire for some time now." Loretta studied Alice with a knowing look that seemed to zero straight in on her heart. "What about you? Any second thoughts about giving your heart to a fisherman?"

A twinge or two, Alice was forced to admit to herself. Aloud she said, "None at all."

"Really? I find that surprising. I always thought that was one of the reasons you left Widow's Cove, because you didn't want to fall into the trap that so many of your ancestors had fallen into. I thought you viewed the sea as your enemy."

Alice shuddered at the reminder. "If I've learned nothing else in the past few years, it's that the heart makes its own choices."

The principal patted her hand. "Indeed it does. I only regret that you came to that wisdom after your parents were gone."

Alice sighed. "I know. I wish I could have told them and begged their forgiveness for making judgments about their choices."

"They bore their own share of the guilt," Loretta reminded her. "They were too hard on you. You were young. You had a right to your choices, as well."

"I know, but I regret that we didn't have a second chance to discuss it more rationally. Maybe I could have made them see how happy I was with the choice I'd made."

"Living with regrets is a waste of time." Loretta gave Alice a sly look. "Have you had any luck making Patrick see that?"

"None at all," Alice admitted.

"I thought not. He's a hard case. It wouldn't surprise me if he took his anger to the grave."

Alice regarded her with surprise. "You don't think there's any hope for a reconciliation with his family?"

"As long as there's breath, there's hope. Keep trying, Alice. I see Patrick's parents from time to time. There was always something a little lost and sad about them, but it's been worse since Patrick left. I don't know the whole story, but it would be a shame if it kept them apart for too long. Mending fences is never easy once pride gets in the way, but without forgiveness, where would any of us be?"

"I know," Alice said. "I agree."

"Then do something about it. He'll listen to you. Once a man's heart opens to love, it's more accepting of a lot of things."

"I don't know that Patrick loves me."

The principal gave her another of those too-knowing looks. "If not, then what was last night about, my dear?"

Alice blushed furiously. "How . . . ?"

A surprising twinkle lit the principal's eyes. "You're wearing your blouse inside out. It's not like you, so I suspect you dressed in a rush this morning."

She grinned at Alice, then strode into her office and firmly shut the door.

Alice stared down at the exposed seams of her blouse and felt as if she might die of embarrassment on the spot. She rushed off to the ladies' room to remedy the telltale mistake before anyone else noticed and the story made its way around town.

She was still completely off-kilter when the day ended and she made her way to Jess's, hoping for at least a glimpse of Patrick before she went home.

At three o'clock the bar was quiet and Molly was sitting in a booth in a darkened corner, her expression brooding. Alice slid in opposite her and studied her worriedly.

"Bad day?" she asked when Molly volunteered nothing, not even a halfhearted greeting.

"Bad enough."

"Want to talk about it?"

"No." She sounded very sure of it, too.

"Sometimes talking helps," Alice pressed.

"And sometimes it's just a waste of breath."

"Now there's a cynical view."

"I have a right," Molly retorted, her tone and her expression unyielding.

"Of course you do, but it's unlike you. People around here know they can count on you for sound advice and a cheery greeting. You'll scare them off if you keep the sour look on your face through happy hour."

Molly feigned a mocking smile. "Will that do?"

"It might fool some, but not most. Talk, Molly."

"I've nothing to say, and if you're going to keep pestering me, I'll be forced to head into the kitchen and start dinner preparations."

"Does that involve sharp knives?"

"Of course."

"Then maybe you should put it off."

Molly gave her a wry look. "Very funny."

"I didn't mean it to be."

Molly started to push herself up, then sank back against the cushions of the booth. The effort was so halfhearted, so counter to everything Alice knew about Molly's usual energy level, that Alice's alarm grew.

"Dammit, Molly, are you sick?"

Molly's gaze turned sad. "Not the way you mean."

"Sick at heart, then?"

She nodded eventually, then cut off all questions by adding firmly, "But I don't want to talk about it."

"It has something to do with Daniel Devaney, though, doesn't it?"

"I said I didn't want to talk about it," Molly repeated, though her voice lacked her usual feistiness.

"Oh, Molly, what did he do to you?" Alice whispered, reaching for her friend's hand.

"Nothing Patrick won't do to you, if you're not careful," Molly said.

The sting of the words was so unexpected that Alice felt as if she'd been slapped. Before she could even think of an adequate response, Molly leaned forward.

"I'm very fond of Patrick," Molly said, her tone filled with urgency. "He's a wonderful man, and he's been a good friend to me, but that's all he's capable of, Alice. That's all either of them are capable of, thanks to those god-awful parents of theirs. Neither of them will ever trust anyone enough to let them into their lives."

Alice refused to believe that was true, at least of Patrick. In fact, she was still convinced that if he could only forgive his parents and make peace with them, his heart would be open to anything. He'd allowed her into his life, hadn't he? That had to mean something.

"You're wrong," she told Molly.

"Am I? What makes you so certain of that? Is it because Patrick slept with you? Because, if you're counting on that to make a difference, I'm here to tell you that it's only the first step on the path to heartbreak."

"You're wrong," Alice said again, unwilling to admit how deeply Molly's words had shaken her. "And it's cruel of you to project whatever happened to you with Daniel onto my relationship with Patrick."

"I'm only trying to warn you because I care about you," Molly said. "And I care about him, as well. Leaving you will hurt him as much as it hurts you, but he'll do it just the same."

"I can't accept that. Keep your warnings to yourself, Molly. I know Patrick. I know what we have together." If she hadn't before last night, she did now, and she didn't intend to let Molly's dire predictions sway her.

Molly merely gave her a sad smile. "I feel sorry for you."

"Why would you feel sorry for me?"

"Because I once felt the same about Daniel. I thought I knew who he was and what we shared. It turned out I knew nothing about him at all."

Alice regretted that she wasn't Ricky Foster's age, that she couldn't clamp her hands over her ears and make nonsense noises to block out Molly's hurtful words.

"Molly, I'm sorry for whatever Daniel did to you. I really am," she replied instead. "But it's got nothing to do with me and Patrick."

"It has everything to do with him," Molly insisted. "They're twins, for goodness' sakes. Identical twins."

"That doesn't mean they see the world exactly alike," Alice said, still fighting for what she'd found with Patrick the night before. She refused to believe it had been nothing more than an illusion, nothing more than incredible sex with no meaning behind it.

"Do you think because Patrick broke free of his

parents after he and Daniel found out about their brothers that he's somehow more well adjusted than Daniel?" Molly asked.

"No." The opposite, in fact, though Alice wasn't ready to admit that, not when Molly was in this odd mood.

"Well, I'm glad you can see that much, at least," Molly said with evident relief.

"One day he'll make peace with them," Alice said.

Molly stared at her. "For a minute, there, I thought there was some hope for you, but now I see that you're delusional, after all."

"He will," Alice insisted.

"And then what? The Devaneys will all live happily ever after?"

"Yes."

"No," Molly said flatly. "You've been spending too much time with five-year-olds. This isn't a fairy tale, Alice. It's real life, and some betrayals are too huge. You're not going to have some picture-perfect family to make up for the one you lost."

Once again the sting of the words had the power to take her breath away. For Molly to be so harsh, so unbelievably cruel, her own pain had to be overwhelming. Alice wished she could look Daniel Devaney in the eyes and tell him what a heartless fool he was for whatever he'd done to Molly. She doubted she could fix this, though. Molly was probably right about one thing—some betrayals *were* too huge.

"I'm so sorry he hurt you so badly," she told Molly. "One of these days you'll meet someone else and forget all about Daniel."

Molly gave her a sad, tired smile. "If only it were that easy," she said.

Before Alice could respond, Molly visibly pulled herself together and stood up.

"I'm sorry you caught the brunt of my foul mood," she told Alice. "I'm usually better at keeping it under wraps."

"Why not today?"

"An anniversary of sorts," Molly said.

"You can tell me, you know. And I can even manage to hold my tongue, if you're not anxious for my advice."

Molly laughed at that. "Now it would almost be worth testing you on that, but I have things to do in the kitchen. If you want to make yourself useful, there's an inventory checklist for the liquor that I meant to get done this afternoon."

Alice nodded. "I imagine I can count a few bottles and write the totals down without messing up. Jess always left that to me, because you were too easily distracted."

Molly chuckled. "He did at that. I'd forgotten. Your parents would have had a fit had they known that my grandfather was letting you near the whiskey and teaching you to play poker."

"Which was exactly why I loved coming here so much," Alice told her. "I think I already had a well-developed rebellious streak, even in grade school."

"You did, indeed," Molly concurred. "That's why it's such a wonder that they're letting you teach at that very school. Now, get busy, before Patrick wanders in and distracts you all over again."

Alice watched her friend go into the kitchen, then sighed. She would give anything to ease Molly's pain, but how could she, when Molly wouldn't even reveal what the problem was beyond an obviously bitter breakup?

Of course, Patrick probably knew the details, she realized as she found the inventory sheet and began counting the stock behind the bar. And she knew all sorts of clever ways for making him talk. She'd have to put a few of them to good use later tonight.

Chapter Thirteen

Patrick found Alice hunkered down and bent over in a fascinatingly provocative position when he walked into Jess's. Fortunately the bar was empty, or he'd no doubt have had to bust the chops of a few male patrons eager to get an eyeful of her delectable backside. Since they were alone, he walked up behind her, snagged her around the waist and pulled her against him.

She gasped in surprise, then twisted to face him. "Trying to take advantage of me?" She seemed more intrigued than upset by the possibility.

He grinned. "Looked to me as if you were waiting for me to come along."

She feigned a scowl. "Hardly. I was doing inventory to help Molly out."

"Remind me to have you come by the boat and take inventory for me sometime," he said.

She gave him a look that had his pulse jumping. "I'm almost finished here," she told him, a deliberate taunt in her voice. "Just what do you have to be inventoried?"

"Oh, I think you'd find it more interesting than this," he assured her.

"Ask me again after dinner," she suggested, wriggling free in a way designed to torment him some more. "The special's herb-roasted chicken. I've been smelling it for the past hour, and I'm not leaving here till I've had some."

"Then let me get our order in while you finish up here. Where is Molly, by the way?"

"Hiding in the kitchen," Alice said, her expression suddenly sobering. "She's having a bad day, Patrick. Worse than usual. Any idea why?"

Patrick glanced at the calendar on the wall behind the bar, then muttered a curse and shoved into the kitchen without another word to Alice. He trusted her to stay where she was and give him a few minutes alone to offer whatever comfort he could to Molly. He should have remembered the day without a reminder from Alice. He always made it a point to stick close by when this particular anniversary came around.

When he burst into the kitchen, Molly glanced up from the pot of mashed potatoes she was whipping. Her face was streaked with tears. She swiped at them ineffectively, her movements jerky and impatient.

"Unusual way to salt the potatoes, don't you think?" he said gently.

"I'm not going to discuss my tears with you," Molly said, sniffing. "They'll pass. They always do."

"Oh, Molly," Patrick said, drawing her into his arms and letting her renewed flow of tears dampen his shirt as she finally relaxed in his arms. "Sometimes I could string my brother up from the tallest tree in town and flog him." He felt her mouth curve into a smile against his shoulder. "You like that idea, do you? Just say the word and I'll do it. You always were a bloodthirsty little thing."

"Only where Daniel's concerned," she said, her voice catching. She pulled back and met his gaze. "It's been three years. I don't know why it still catches me off guard like this."

"It's been longer than that since I discovered the truth about my folks and left home. The pain of their betrayal still surprises me sometimes. It's as fresh as if it happened yesterday," he said. "There's no timetable on something like this. Your heart will heal when it's ready."

"And yours?"

He avoided her gaze. "Mine's cold as stone."

"If that's true, then you shouldn't be with Alice," she chided, her expression worried.

Patrick sighed. "You're probably right, but I can't walk away from her, Molly. And I don't want to discuss my relationship with her with you, not till I've got it figured out for myself."

"We're quite the happy little trio tonight, all of us with our secrets and forbidden topics," Molly said with a rare touch of bitterness. "They could make a TV soap opera about Widow's Cove, with our lives as the central plotline."

"Why not suggest it and make us all rich?" Patrick said. "There should be some benefit to going through the kind of anguish you and I and Alice have been through."

"You'd have to do it," she said. "I can't write worth a damn."

"Neither can I," Patrick lamented. "Oh, well, it was just an idea."

Molly sighed. "I could sure use a drink."

"You're entitled," he said.

"Which is why I won't have one," she said. "It would be too easy to use liquor to numb the pain. And in the end, what does that accomplish?"

Patrick was hit with a sudden flash of insight. "Which is why Alice is out there poking through your liquor stock, isn't it?"

She nodded. "I started doing the inventory, but the temptation was too great. When Alice offered to help out, I grabbed at the chance to turn the chore over to her."

"Good for you. Seeing you upset worries her. She needs to be doing something to help."

"I know, but I can't explain it to her," Molly said. "You'd better get back out there before she starts to wonder what we're up to in here. Alice has never been one to ignore her curiosity for long. She's been pestering me about Daniel all afternoon, but I refuse to discuss him."

Patrick studied Molly's face. Her tears had dried, but there was still unbearable sadness in her eyes, and his brother had put it there. He felt partly responsible for that. He should have done a better job of protecting her, but no one had been able to get through to Molly once she'd fallen under Daniel's spell.

"You sure you're going to be okay?" he asked.

"I'm not sure of much," she said, "but I am sure of that. You and me, we're survivors, Patrick, you in spite of being a Devaney, me because of one."

"Don't ever forget that, Molly, not even for a second."

She gave him a forced smile. "Get on out of here—the potatoes are going cold. I'll have to reheat them in the microwave, and you know how that goes against my grain. I'll bring your dinners out in a minute. I imagine you both want the special."

"The special and a smile on your face."

"I can promise one but not the other. I'll do my best, though."

He gave her a long, lingering look, then finally nodded, satisfied with what he saw. "Five minutes more of hiding out and not a second longer," he warned. "You don't want me back in here."

"You're right about that," she said. "You get in the way."

He left her with some regret and went in search of Alice, who'd poured them each a beer and found a booth where the light was dim.

"That took a while," she said, searching his face. "Is Molly okay?"

"She's fine."

Alice looked skeptical. "She's not fine, Patrick."

"She will be," he insisted.

"Can't you tell me what happened? She's my friend, too. I want to help."

"She'll tell you what she wants you to know. It's enough that she understands you care," he said, then reached for her hand and pressed a kiss against her knuckles. "Let's talk about this inventory we're going to do at my place tonight."

"You know, if you keep secrets from me, there's a good chance we won't *be* at your place," she told him tartly. "Not tonight. Not ever."

He pulled away from her and sat back, feeling his defenses slip into place the way they always did when a woman tried to back him into a corner, however innocently. It didn't seem to matter that the argument was over Molly's secrets and not his own.

"Your choice," he said.

Hurt flashed in her eyes. "Would it be that easy for you to stop this, Patrick?" she asked. "Could you let me turn my back and walk away?"

He deliberately shrugged. "Like I said, it's your choice."

She kept her gaze steady on him, then sighed. "In that case, I think I'd better do just that and go home," she said, slipping out of the booth. "Tell Molly I'm sorry about dinner. Not that either of you will apparently give a damn whether I'm here or not. It's nice that you have each other's shoulders to cry on."

The implication that they had deliberately shut her out of something important cut through him. Patrick wanted to reach out and stop her. One heartfelt word of apology was all it would have taken, one touch. But he couldn't make himself do it. Instead, he watched her leave and told himself the ache in his heart had nothing at all to do with her going. He almost believed it, too. After all, over the years he'd gotten damn good at lying to himself.

Alice glanced up from the notes she was making for end-of-the-year report cards and saw Patrick coming across the school yard, a bouquet of lilacs in hand. It had been four days, four endless days, since she'd last laid eyes on him. Her heart did an automatic flip even though she'd vowed at least a hundred times to steel herself against the effect he had on her. She'd almost convinced herself that Molly was right, there was nothing to be gained by clinging to a false hope that Patrick would change.

Walking out of Jess's, waiting as she crossed the room for Patrick to give even the tiniest sign that he didn't want her to go, had almost killed her. She'd seen it as evidence that Patrick might enjoy sleeping with her, might even have feelings for her on some level, but he wasn't letting her into his heart, not really, not if he could let her go so easily. It saddened her that Molly knew him better than she did. And she was just the teensiest bit jealous that the two of them had a history she knew nothing about.

Outside the window, he had disappeared from view, which could only mean he was in the building. She listened for the sound of his footsteps in the silent hallway, trying to brace herself against the impact he always had on her. She needed to be cool and distant and unapproachable. Unfortunately, she didn't have the vaguest idea how she was going to pull off such a lie.

Suddenly he was there, without a whisper of sound to announce him, only the faint scent of lilacs to capture her attention. He filled the doorway, looking oddly uncertain as he waited for her to give some indication of whether he was welcome. She said nothing. She couldn't gather the words or her thoughts. None of the heated words she'd mentally flung at him over the past few days were coming to her now. She was too darned glad to see him.

"Want me to leave?" he asked eventually.

"What I want and what I should want are two different things," she told him candidly, then threw his own words back at him. "I guess that makes it your choice."

"Then I'll stay," he said, stepping into the room. "That's what you should have done at Jess's, Alice. You should have stayed."

"Why, when it was plain you didn't care which I

did?" She frowned at him. "Don't try making what happened my fault, Patrick."

"I cared," he said. "I'm just lousy at saying it. I'm even worse at looking ahead more than a minute or two."

She sighed then, noting that he'd opted to ignore the fact that their fight had to do with Molly's secrets. Since he was focusing on his own mistakes, she would, too.

"Do you think that will ever change?" she asked.

"I doubt it."

"I see. So where does that leave us?"

"Can you try to hear what I'm not saying as well as what comes out of my mouth? Can you take here and now?" he asked plaintively. "Can you not worry about the future?"

How could she, when she wanted a future with this man so desperately? But he wasn't offering one, not yet anyway. Once again he was giving her the choice of taking him as he was . . . or not. She had a feeling what she said and did in the next few minutes would make or break any chance they had.

She blinked away the tears that threatened and faced him. "Are those lilacs for me?"

He nodded.

"I suppose I should put them in some water." She got to her feet, found an old vase in a cupboard, filled it with water, then took the flowers, burying her face in them before setting them on a corner of her desk.

"Is there an answer in there I'm missing?" he asked eventually, regarding her warily.

She turned slowly, lifted her gaze to meet his. "The classroom is a little inappropriate for my answer. How about your place?"

Relief spread across his face, and she took heart at the sight of it.

"How fast can you gather up those papers?" he asked.

"I may as well leave them here," she said, grabbing only her purse. "Something tells me I won't be getting to them any time over the weekend."

He grinned. "Not if I have my way."

It wasn't just about the fabulous sex, Patrick told himself a thousand times over the weekend, as he and Alice shut themselves away on his boat. He wasn't using her. He would never do that to her.

But he couldn't bring himself to define what it *was* about. He'd never let a woman get this close, never felt so needy and out of sorts when she was away. The four days before he'd swallowed his pride and gone after Alice had been the most miserable he'd spent since the early days after he'd left home.

"You know," she said, staring at him across his tiny kitchen table. "I really should go home and get a change of clothes."

"Why, when I'd only make you take them off?" he teased.

She grinned. "Maybe that's why. I'm thinking something with lots and lots of tiny buttons, so you can fumble and be adorable as you try to undo them."

"You think I have the patience for that? I'm more likely to rip them apart."

"That could be interesting, too. I'll make it something *old* with tiny buttons."

"Forget it. I like the way you look in my shirt. I had no idea that an old T-shirt could look that sexy on someone."

"If it's that enticing, why am I still dressed in it?"

"Sometimes anticipation is every bit as important as the sex," he said, realizing it was true. He liked the slow buildup of heat. He liked knowing where it would lead, knowing how her body would respond. He liked the teasing, the exchange of smoldering looks and lingering caresses.

But even as he thought of his own amazing level of contentment, Alice's grin faltered.

"Patrick, are you sure you're not getting tired of having me underfoot?"

He stared at her in shock. "Do I act as if I'm bored?"

"No, but it's not as if you're used to sharing these quarters with another person."

He studied her with a narrowed gaze. "What are you really saying, Alice? Is being shut up here on the boat with me getting on your nerves?"

"Don't be ridiculous."

Relief washed over him. He hadn't realized how desperately he'd begun to want this to work. If she'd said she wanted to go home, he wasn't sure how he would have reacted.

"Okay, then," he said.

"But I will need to get back to my place tonight," she told him.

Immediately he tensed. "Why?"

"I have school tomorrow. There's no way I can put that off, and I can't very well wear the same thing I had on on Friday."

As reasonable as the explanation was, it made his stomach tighten. He was the one who wanted things to be temporary, but hearing her making plans to take off upset him in ways he couldn't explain.

"Patrick?"

"What?"

"You do know I can't just stay here forever, right? It's not as if we've sailed away to some idyllic island. We both have responsibilities."

There was that word again—*forever*. He seized on it and nothing else. Over the past couple of days, the word and its implications had lost some of their power to terrify him. "Of course I know that."

"You could come to my place," she suggested casually. "It would make it easier during the week. That is, if you wanted to."

"I don't know," he said, the cautious words

239

coming out before he could consider them. It was an automatic, knee-jerk response. His turf was one thing, hers was something else. He thought of that cozy little cottage, and it made his palms sweat. Being there had made him want things that he'd learned couldn't be trusted—a home, a family.

"Think about it," she said. "And school will be out soon. I could stay here then, if you'd prefer it. I could even go out fishing with you."

A part of him liked the idea of sharing his life with her that way. Another part was terrified. All this talk about tomorrow and the day after tomorrow and beyond was treading on turf he normally avoided like the plague. He didn't do plans. He didn't look into the future. Forever might not be as frightening as it had once been, but it was still off-limits. He wasn't ready to toss all of his rules and common sense out the window, just because the mere thought of them no longer panicked him.

"Let me know when you're ready to go and I'll take you home," he said tightly, ignoring all of her bright and cheerful plans for the summer.

There was no mistaking the quick rise of hurt in Alice's eyes. That, of course, was the problem. He was going to hurt her eventually. There was no question about it. He'd been deluding himself when he'd tried to pretend that they could take things one day at a time. Alice was a forever woman. She had every right to expect permanence

240

and commitment, but he didn't believe in either one.

"Whenever you want me to go, just say the word," she said stiffly.

"I don't *want* you to go," he retorted, more exasperated with himself than with her. He was the one who wasn't making any sense. "I just think it's for the best."

"Because you're scared," she guessed.

"Because I'm smart," he corrected.

"And if I disagree about what's smart?"

"You're entitled to your opinion."

She stood up in that oversize T-shirt of his that skimmed her thighs and managed to emphasize her curves. He expected her to flounce from the room, but instead she rounded the table to sit in his lap. She draped an arm loosely around his neck and skimmed a finger along his stubbled cheek.

"It is my opinion," she said, "that we're doing entirely too much talking all of a sudden. It always gets us into trouble. You get that worried frown on your forehead." She pressed a kiss to the place in question. "And lines right here," she added, kissing the down-turned corners of his mouth.

"We can't go through life making love whenever we butt heads," he said, trying to maintain his grip on reason even as she tried to torment him with sneaky little kisses.

"Can you think of a better way to remind ourselves of what's really important?" She looked him in the eye. "I love you, Patrick. All the rest of it—" she waved her hand dismissively "—we'll work it out."

"Alice," he began, but the protest died on his lips when she covered his mouth with hers.

He sighed and gave himself up to the desire instantly slamming through him. Maybe she did know what was important, after all. He could wrestle with his doubts when she wasn't around to torment him.

"This thing between you and Alice, is it serious?" Molly asked Patrick several days after Alice had gone back to her place.

He frowned at the question. "What thing?" he asked, being deliberately obtuse. This was not a conversation he intended to pursue, not with Molly. He thought he'd made that clear to her.

Molly scowled at him. "Oh, please. Half the town knows the two of you never left your boat all weekend. Only an idiot would assume she was helping you work on the engine or clean the galley for that long."

Patrick bit back a curse. He'd forgotten what small towns were like when people got hold of a juicy piece of gossip. He didn't give a damn for himself, but it couldn't be good for Alice to have people talking about the two of them. Maybe if he'd put an engagement ring on her finger, it would dispel the talk, but that was out of the question.

"Sweetheart, you know nothing I do is ever serious," he told Molly, adopting his devil-may-care tone of old.

Her gaze narrowed. "Does Alice understand that?"

"Of course," he said at once.

"Does she *really?*" Molly persisted. "Because if you hurt her, Patrick Devaney, I swear I'll come out on that pitiful dock of yours and set fire to it *and* your boat."

She would do it, too. He didn't have any doubts about that. Molly had a mile-wide protective streak when it came to her friends, and a built-in aversion to the way Devaney men treated women. He'd always been glad to count himself among the friends, despite his last name. Obviously, though, she considered Alice to be the friend most in need of protection now . . . from him.

"Look, I'll talk to her, okay? I'll make sure we're both on the same page," he said. He recalled how the last time he'd tried to have that conversation with Alice it hadn't gone so well. She'd seemed to hear only what she wanted to hear, dismissing everything else.

"When?" Molly pressed.

"Tonight," he promised.

"What's wrong with now?"

"She's at school."

Molly clearly wasn't satisfied with his response. Hands on hips, she asked, "Why put it off, Patrick?

The kids are only there a half day today. The teachers are all alone in their classrooms grading papers and stuff in the afternoon. Knowing Alice, she had all that done days ago and is sitting there bored to tears and staring at the walls."

"Molly, you can't actually expect me to have a conversation like this with her in her classroom. It's totally inappropriate," he said. Besides, if he kept showing up in Alice's classroom, that was going to set off its own round of speculation. He'd run into Loretta Dowd on his last visit, and she'd given him an approving grin that had completely rattled him.

"It's not an ideal situation, no, but if you put it off, you'll just think of some other excuse. I know you, Patrick. You'd rather run than stick around and settle things. Isn't that what you did with your folks?"

"Leave my folks out of this," he retorted heatedly. "I'll talk to Alice. I'll spell things out for her one more time, but I'll decide when and where. This is none of your business."

"I'm making it my business. I like her, Patrick. And she's in way over her head with you. She's in love with you."

He wanted to deny that, but the echo of Alice saying those very words had rung in his head all week long. The words had meant more to him than he wanted to admit, but he wasn't about to let Molly know that.

"So what if she is?" he asked, his tone cavalier.

Molly scowled at him. "Do you honestly need me to answer that?"

Patrick sighed. "No. I'll talk to her."

There was just one problem . . . once he talked to Alice, really talked to her, things might never be the same. And for the first time in his life he didn't want to lose the feelings he'd discovered in her arms, feelings he'd never imagined himself capable of.

Chapter Fourteen

Even if she hadn't been taken aback earlier in the day when Patrick had sent a written summons to her classroom, Alice would have known something was wrong the minute she stepped aboard the *Katie G.*

Patrick was waiting for her on the deck, a brooding expression on his face and a beer in his hand. He didn't look especially happy to see her. The fact that he'd been avoiding her most of the week only added to her alarm.

She hesitated when he said nothing, then finally sat down next to him and put her feet up on the railing. The afternoon sun was warm on her face, but the breeze held a promising hint of rain. There would be a storm before nightfall, no question about it. And she had a feeling there would be one on board between her and Patrick even sooner.

She finally dared a glance in his direction. "Is everything okay, Patrick? Have you heard something from your brothers in Boston? Or from Daniel or your folks?"

"No, it's nothing like that."

"What then?"

"We need to talk."

Something inside her froze at the tone in his voice. Those words never meant anything good. "About?"

"Us."

She'd been anticipating this for days now. In some ways she was surprised it had been so long in coming. As much as she'd wanted to pretend that Molly's warning was misplaced, she hadn't been able to forget it. Patrick intended to dump her before things got complicated, or, rather, any *more* complicated. She'd told him she loved him and that had been the kiss of death. It would be with a lot of men, but especially with a man who had the kind of trust issues Patrick had. And he was too damned noble to let her go on loving him when he was convinced he could never love her back.

Her pride immediately kicked in. She had no intention of being the one dumped. She looked him straight in the eye. "Okay. Are you going to start or shall I?"

He stared at her in surprise, as if it had never occurred to him that she might have an opinion on that subject. "You, by all means," he said politely.

"You're going to say that what's been going on between us has gotten out of hand, that I might be misinterpreting what it means, and that you never intended for it to get serious." She met his gaze. "How am I doing so far?"

He scowled at her. "Am I that predictable?"

"You are when it comes to relationships. When they get too difficult, you run. I suspect you never even allow most relationships to get to that point."

"Dammit, you're the second person today to say

247

something like that to me. I'm getting sick of it."

"You heard it first from Molly, I imagine," she said, trying not to be angry at a friend who only thought she was looking out for Alice's best interests by pushing Patrick to be honest with her. "I also suspect she's the one who told you that you needed to spell things out for me for my sake."

"She thinks I'll hurt you," he said defensively.

"What do you think?"

He met her gaze, his expression miserable. "That she's probably right, eventually I will hurt you, Alice. It's what I do."

"You could stop the pattern. All you have to do is quit running," she countered.

"Simple as that?" he said, his expression wry.

"Why not? I've never hurt you or given you any reason to distrust me. That was your parents. And from what you've said, you never really gave them a chance to explain why they did what they did to your older brothers or why they kept it from you and Daniel. You had one conversation that caught them completely off guard, then turned your back on them—and on your brother, who's as much a victim in this situation as you are—and ran."

Alice met his turbulent gaze. "Believe me, Patrick, I know all about running. I did the same thing. I shut my parents out of my life because of one hurtful argument. I made one more halfhearted attempt to reconcile by sending them that invitation to my graduation, and then I wrote them off.

Before I realized how ridiculous that was, what a waste, it was too late. I'll regret that for the rest of my life."

"I'm sorry," he said.

"So am I." She regarded him with a penetrating look. "Let me ask you something. Has being alone made you happy? Or has it only made you feel safe?" She held up her hand when he seemed about to speak. "Don't answer me now. I want you to think long and hard about that when I'm gone. I knew the risks when I got involved with you. I don't know about you, but I've felt more alive lately than I have in years. In my opinion, that's a helluva lot better than safe and alone. You can protect your heart, Patrick. Or you can live. I protected myself once and it cost me everything. Never again. I'm going to live my life as if there's no tomorrow."

She stood up, leaned down and pressed a quick kiss to the grim line of his mouth, then walked away before the tears that were threatening could fall.

Patrick stared after Alice and cursed himself for letting her walk away yet again. She'd caught him completely off guard when she'd taken the decision to call it quits out of his hands. She did that a lot—in fact, she had a way of taking him by surprise that should have made him nuts. Instead it filled him with anticipation. It also made him ashamed that he wasn't nearly as brave as she was. Not only was she brave enough to go, but she'd been brave enough to take a risk on staying if only he'd met her halfway.

But no more. She'd left no doubt in his mind that she was finished. She'd seen the handwriting on the wall, handwriting he'd scrawled there in big, bold, unmistakable letters, and had wisely decided to cut her losses.

He should be dancing for joy at being free of a commitment he'd been incapable of making in the first place. Instead all he felt was the sense that he'd lost something precious, something he'd never be able to replace.

He would have gone to Jess's and gotten blind, stinking drunk, but he wasn't sure he wanted to listen to any more of Molly's comments on his love life. He sure as hell didn't want to argue with her over whether or not what had happened was for the best. Of course it was. But he didn't have to like it.

He should take his boat out to sea and let the demands of fishing tax his muscles and clear his head, but the prospect held no appeal.

Ironically, he had a sudden urge to call Daniel. His twin had always been able to put things into perspective for him when it came to women. Not that Daniel had much wisdom in that area of his own life—the mess he'd made of things with Molly was testament to that. But when it came to

Patrick, Daniel had always seen things more clearly.

Patrick almost reached for the phone, then caught himself. He could make that call only if he was willing to take everything that went along with it. He would have to reconcile with his brother, and that would be only one step away from letting his folks back into his life. He almost did it anyway, but the weight of all that old baggage kept his hand off the phone.

For the first time since he'd moved away, Patrick felt unbearably lonely. He'd been alone before and never minded it. Today, though, it made his heart ache. With Alice he'd had a taste of something incredible. He could call it companionship or sex and demean it, but he was honest enough not to do that. What he'd shared with her had been love in its purest, most incredible form, and he'd let it slip through his fingers.

"Hey, Patrick. You look as if you've lost your best friend," Ray Stover said, calling out to him from the end of the dock.

Grateful for the interruption, Patrick waved the older man on board. "What brings you by, Ray?"

"I wanted to thank you again for coming to my rescue." He handed over a package wrapped in bright-yellow paper and tied with string. "A little something from Janey. Judging from the shape of it, it's probably one of the sweaters she knits when I'm not around. The truth is, they're usually too

251

big and she tends to drop a lot of stitches, so I won't be offended if you hang it on the back of the door and forget about it."

Patrick laughed as he untied the bow around the package and opened it to find a dark-green sweater that was every bit as large and unevenly made as Ray had predicted. "Nice color," he said, seizing on the one thing Janey had gotten exactly right.

Ray grinned. "That's very diplomatic, Patrick. I'll tell her you love the color and she'll be pleased as punch."

"Is that the only reason you came by, to deliver Janey's thank-you gift?"

Ray looked sheepish. "To tell you the truth, I'm going stir-crazy around the house. Janey's already lost her enthusiasm for having me underfoot—she says I disrupt her routine. I thought I might take you up on that invitation to go out fishing—that is, if you're heading out this afternoon."

"I was just debating whether to try to get in a couple of hours before nightfall," Patrick said. "I'd be glad of the company."

Ray leaped to his feet with an agility that belied his years and began untying the boat from its moorings. Patrick moved more slowly, amused by the man's enthusiasm.

"Something tells me you're going to be looking around to buy a new boat one of these days," he told Ray.

"Not as long as you'll let me help you out from time to time. I'm retired for good. That's the way it has to be," Ray said, not sounding as unhappy about it as he had when the decision had first been taken out of his hands.

"Is that because it's what your wife wants?"

"No, it's because it's what's right for the two of us. That's what marriage is about, son, making compromises for the good of both of you."

"Don't you both wind up losing that way?"

"Only if that's the way you choose to see it," Ray told him.

"Is there another way?" Patrick asked, genuinely curious.

"You can see it as both of you giving up a little bit for the good of what you have together. Then you both come out winners—though, to be honest, as soon as you start thinking in terms of winners and losers you're in trouble." He gave Patrick a speculative look. "Is that what was on your mind when I got here a bit ago? You and that pretty young teacher at odds over something?"

"In a way."

"Is what she wants unreasonable?"

Patrick wasn't sure how to answer. She wanted him to love her enough to forget about the past. She wanted him to trust in their love. The requests weren't unreasonable. Maybe just a little unrealistic, given where he was coming from.

"No," he told Ray eventually.

"Do you want to lose her? Is clinging to your position more important than keeping her in your life?"

"No," he said more quickly.

Ray grinned. "Well, then, I think you have your answer."

Patrick sighed. He had an answer, all right. He just had no idea at all about how to put it into practice. How could he compromise a little bit when it came to letting go of the past? There was no way to open the door just a crack to his parents and Daniel. It had to be all or nothing.

The same with acting on his feelings for Alice. If he went back to her, he had to be prepared to love her with all his heart. He had to allow himself to be vulnerable to her. He couldn't protectively close himself off to his feelings without shortchanging both of them.

But one thing was certain, he didn't want to go on like this. He'd had a taste of what a full life could be, and anything else was unacceptable.

Alice was attacking the weeds in her garden when she heard the doorbell ring. She stayed right where she was. There was no one she wanted to see. There hadn't been anyone she wanted to see for days now. She grabbed another handful of weeds and tugged viciously, then flung them over her shoulder.

"What was that for?" Molly demanded irritably.

Alice sighed and turned around, only to see her friend wiping traces of dirt and weeds from her face and the front of her blouse.

"Sorry," Alice said without any real sincerity in her tone. She was almost as furious with Molly these days as she was with Patrick. She knew that Molly was behind that little talk Patrick had insisted they needed to have. Even though Alice had gotten in the first word, the handwriting had been on the wall from the instant she stepped aboard his boat. Molly might have meddled out of affection for both of them, but she'd set off a chain reaction that had been as painful as anything that might have come down the road.

"Yeah, I can tell how sorry you are," Molly replied.

"What do you expect from me?"

"Why don't we start with an explanation of where you've been lately?"

"At school, working here in the garden, around town."

"Just not at Jess's," Molly concluded.

"Pretty much."

"Avoiding me or avoiding Patrick?"

"Both."

"Why?"

"As if you don't know," Alice accused.

"I don't," Molly said. "Patrick's been making himself scarce, too."

"Then go chase him down and try all your questions on him. Maybe he'll be more receptive to them than I am."

Molly answered by sitting down on a chaise longue and stretching out. She looked as if she had no intention of leaving anytime soon. Removing her sunglasses, she turned her face up to the sun. "Nice day, isn't it?"

Alice rocked back on her heels and sighed. "You're not going to go away, are you?"

"Not until I get the answers I came for."

"Okay, here it is in a nutshell. Patrick called me over to break up with me. I broke up with him first. You were right. It wasn't going to work. You got us both to face that fact. Happy?"

"No, I am not happy," Molly said, her own expression glum. "How could I be, when you're so obviously miserable?"

"I'm not miserable," Alice retorted heatedly. "I'm furious."

"With Patrick?"

"And with you. You were so sure we couldn't make it work. I know you were bugging him to be straight with me because you care about me, but all you did was to back him into making a decision before any decision needed to be made."

Molly looked her in the eye. "How long were you willing to wait?"

"As long as it took," Alice insisted.

"Really? Then you don't care about having chil-

256

dren? You were willing to put your whole life on hold while he wrestles with all those demons on his back?"

"Yes."

"Even if after all that waiting around and wasting your life, you could still lose him?"

"Even then," Alice said.

"You're crazy," Molly said flatly. "You'd wind up hating him and blaming me for not stepping in sooner."

"It was my decision, Molly, not yours. You took it out of my hands."

"I merely wanted you both to face the truth before it was too late."

"What truth? I'm in love with him. Is that the truth you meant?" she retorted vehemently. "That's not going to go away just because it might be more sensible if I weren't."

Molly stared at her in shock. "If you're in love with him, really in love with him, then why the hell did you break up with him?"

"Because it was what he wanted."

"So basically you just let him off the hook?"

"It was easier on both of us to get it over with."

"Why make it easy for him, Alice? Why not make him squirm and say the words?"

Alice frowned at the hint that she'd somehow taken the easy way out. She especially resented it coming from Molly, who'd set all this in motion. "What purpose would that have served?"

"If it had been hard for him to let go, he might have had to question whether it was what he really wanted. Now he thinks it's what *you* wanted. You've given him one more reason to believe that love isn't strong enough to weather anything."

"That's not fair," Alice said, though she couldn't help wondering if that wasn't exactly what she'd done.

"One of you needed to fight for what you had. It was never likely to be Patrick—that left you. I thought you understood that, Alice."

"Maybe you should have explained the rules before you started meddling."

"I didn't think I needed to. You were so certain of how you felt, of how Patrick felt. I expected you to fight like a banshee to keep him."

Alice studied Molly speculatively. "Did you fight for Daniel, Molly?"

"No," Molly admitted. "I don't know that it would have changed anything, but I'll still regret it till the day I die."

Alice forgot for a moment how angry she was about Molly's role in her breakup with Patrick. She reached for her hand. "I'm so sorry. Why don't you do something about it now?"

"It's too late for some things."

"It's never too late," Alice said fiercely.

Molly gave her a sly look. "Then why not go to Patrick and tell him you made a mistake, that you want to fight for a relationship with him?"

Alice frowned at her. "Nice try, but I don't think so."

"Why not? Too much pride?"

Molly's words lingered in Alice's head long after Molly had left to go back to work. Was it just stubborn pride that kept Alice from going to Patrick? Or was it that she'd really finally seen the light and accepted that they couldn't make a go of things?

Images of the way they were together tumbled through her head, like snapshots falling to the floor in a jumble. She wanted to freeze each one, linger over it, but they slipped away in rapid succession, leaving only an overall impression of a joy she'd never expected to find.

Wasn't that worth fighting for? Of course it was, even if it was an uphill battle. She'd painted a rosy picture for herself of the way it could be, of marrying Patrick and making his family her own. But to make that happen, Patrick had to do something he felt was wrong. He had to be willing to let go of the past. If he couldn't, who was she to demand it? No one had been able to make her see the light when it came to her own parents. Why should she expect so much more of him?

Maybe his stubbornness was a mistake he would come to regret . . . or maybe it wasn't. But it was his decision, not hers.

She sighed and stuck her trowel back into the well-worked soil, then brushed the dirt off her hands. Love was a little bit like gardening. It required patience, and sometimes things got messy. But the end results were worth any amount of effort.

Pleased with her analogy, she headed inside to shower and change into something that would send an unmistakable message to Patrick that they weren't over. Not by a long shot.

Chapter Fifteen

For days after Alice had gone, Patrick wrestled with his conscience and his heart. He knew she would never accept a halfway attempt on his part. He had to be ready to face the past before he could stake any claim at all on a future with her.

Because he couldn't bring himself to call Daniel, he picked up the phone and called Ryan, turning to his oldest brother for advice as if it were something he'd been doing his whole life.

"I know what Alice wants from me, but I don't know if I can give it to her," he told Ryan.

"Has it occurred to you that all she really wants is for you to be truly happy?" Ryan asked. "It took me a while to understand that that was what Maggie was after with me. She could see how burying the past had only given it a power over me that it didn't deserve. I wasn't happy. I was just denying my real feelings."

Like Ryan, Patrick wanted to deny that his folks or even Daniel had any power at all over his life, but he knew that wasn't true. Without doing a thing, they were standing squarely between him and the future he wanted with Alice.

"Funny thing about finding the right woman, isn't it?" Ryan said thoughtfully, when Patrick remained silent. "It was Maggie who made me face the fact that I needed to find my family before

I could ever move on. She was right. I still have one more step to take, and there's no way of knowing if it will turn out okay, but once I've taken it, I'll be free of all that weight I've been carrying around inside me. It takes a lot of energy to go on hating people, especially after all these years."

Patrick thought of how consumed he'd been with bitterness and resentment. It had colored the choices he'd made, the lifestyle he'd chosen, even the people he saw and those he avoided because their connections to his folks were too painful. Ryan and Alice were both right. It was no way to live. There was only one way to be rid of it, and it wasn't by burying his head in the sand.

He slowly drew in a deep breath and said, "I could set up a meeting. It wouldn't be the last step for any of us, but it might be a good place to start."

"You set it up, anytime, anyplace," Ryan said at once. "The rest of us will be there. We've been waiting until you were ready. We agreed that it needed to be that way. The Devaney brothers stick together."

Hearing Ryan include him with his older brothers filled Patrick's heart with surprising joy, but because he wasn't entirely certain he was ready to face his folks, at least not without Alice by his side, he said, "I'll start with Daniel. Will that be okay?"

"Start wherever you're comfortable," Ryan said.

"We've all had to make up the rules as we went along, to take things at our own pace and compromise when compromise was called for. I wrestled with all sorts of emotions before I finally made that first call to Sean. It's not as if there's a guidebook we can follow for this kind of thing. There aren't a lot of families who've been through what we've been through."

"Thank God for that," Patrick said with heartfelt sincerity. He pitied anyone who'd been in their shoes. "I'll call you once I've spoken to Daniel."

"Make it soon, little brother. Not for our sake, but for your own—it sounds as if Alice is too special to risk losing."

Patrick smiled. "Yeah, she is. She really is."

Even though Patrick was anxious to put his plan into motion, years of keeping his distance from his family were too ingrained to be overcome in a heartbeat. With almost any other dreaded chore, he would have tackled it at once to put it behind him, but with this, he spent days trying to work up the courage to pick up the phone. He was consoled by Ryan's admission that he'd had a similar struggle before he'd contacted Sean.

Patrick was still tormented by indecision when he heard footsteps on the dock and looked up to see Alice coming toward him with a purposeful stride. She was wearing something designed to make his heart race and his palms sweat. His breath caught in his chest. He was forced to admit that even if she'd been covered from head to toe, he wasn't ready to see her, not yet. He'd wanted to have something to offer her before they talked.

"So, this is where you've been hiding out," she said, as if she'd found him tucked in a cave somewhere.

"It's hardly hiding if I'm on my own boat in broad daylight," he retorted. "You must not have been looking too hard. What's up?"

"I actually had a request for your presence at the kindergarten graduation ceremony next week. Ricky Foster would be honored if you'd attend."

Patrick bit back a grin. "Is that so? They hold graduation ceremonies for kindergarten? Why is that?"

"We've found it motivates them and gives them a greater sense of purpose when they start first grade and things get more serious," she explained.

"I see. Was there some reason Ricky couldn't come over here and ask me himself?"

"I agreed to do it. He seems to think I might have more influence where you're concerned."

"Really? Where would he get an idea like that?"

She blushed just enough to put some color into her pale cheeks. "Around town."

Patrick flinched at the idea that they were still the subject of gossip, especially as now people were probably speculating about why they were no longer seeing each other. "I'm sorry."

"Don't be. I think it's rather sweet that he's joined in the matchmaking. He might be better at it than Molly."

Patrick grinned. "Yeah, her skills in that department could definitely use some work."

"So, will you come to graduation?" she persisted.

"Sure. Where and when?"

"The school auditorium on Monday. Ten o'clock."

"I'll be there," he promised.

Alice looked as if she weren't quite sure what to do next. She finally met his gaze. "Any chance you can have dinner tonight?"

As desperately as he wanted to say yes, knowing how irresistible she was in that slinky sundress, he shook his head. "I don't think so."

"I guess that would be too much like a date," she said, "and we're not doing that anymore."

Because she looked so miserable, he wanted to tell her everything about how he was trying to put his life back together just for her, but he didn't want to get her hopes up in case he failed.

"It's not that. I just have some things I need to do."

"Sure," she said, her skepticism plain. "No problem, I'll see you at school on Monday."

"Maybe we can talk after the ceremony," he suggested. "You going to be around?"

She nodded. "There's always a lot left to do after the kids finally leave."

"I'll see you then."

"Fine."

She looked so dejected as she began to walk away that he called out to her. "Alice?"

She turned to look at him.

"It's a date, okay?"

A faint smile touched her lips. "It's a date."

"And you could wear that dress again, if you wanted to. It takes my breath away."

The smile that spread across her face was his reward for being honest for once and saying what was in his heart.

As soon as she'd gone, Patrick knew what he had to do. He went inside the boat, picked up his phone and dialed the once-familiar number of his brother's office in Portland.

Daniel answered, as always, on the very first ring, but he sounded distracted.

"Daniel, it's Patrick."

Silence greeted him, then a long sigh. "Hey, bro, what's up?"

Just like that, the years of separation faded away. "We have some catching up to do," Patrick told him. "Can we get together?"

"Anytime," Daniel said at once.

"Over the weekend, maybe Sunday around one?"

"That works for me. Where?"

"Here, on my boat." He needed this first meeting to be on his turf, not Daniel's.

"Want to tell me what this is about?"

"I'll explain when I see you. There are some people I want you to meet. I think you'll really like them."

"If they're friends of yours, I'm sure I will," Daniel said. "Or are we talking about a woman, Patrick? Are you getting married? I've heard some rumors about you and a teacher at the elementary school."

"Maybe one of these days," he admitted. "But this isn't about that, not the way you mean, anyway. Just be here on Sunday, okay?"

"I'll be there," Daniel promised. "I'm glad you called. I've been waiting a long time."

"I know," Patrick said with a sigh. "Too long."

"Something's going on with Patrick," Molly told Alice on Saturday. "Any idea what it is?"

"Beats me. I had the same sense that something was up when I saw him yesterday. What tipped you off?"

"He's just hauled enough coleslaw and potato salad down to his boat to feed an army, along with hamburger patties and an entire keg of beer."

"Sounds as if he's having a party," Alice said slowly, then gasped. "What if he's getting together with his brothers?" She met Molly's gaze. "*All* of them."

"Even Daniel?" Molly asked, an unmistakable hitch in her voice.

"That would be my guess. Do you know of anyone else Patrick would invite for a party?"

"To be honest, no," Molly said. "At least, not without telling me about it. Daniel's the only person he wouldn't want me to know was around. If he's being secretive, then Daniel has to be involved. I think maybe I'll close the bar tomorrow and go hiking somewhere."

Alice studied her friend's miserable expression. "Wouldn't you rather stay here and see who turns up?"

Molly shook her head. "I'll leave the spying to you."

"I'm not going to spy," Alice denied heatedly.

Molly grinned then. "More than one stroll past that dock and it's considered spying. Get a good look the first time."

Alice grinned back at her. "Believe me, I intend to."

Patrick was as nervous as if this were the first time he'd ever thrown a party. Of course, it was the first time he'd ever held one for his brothers. He checked the food at least a hundred times, counted napkins and plates, rearranged the bowls of potato salad and coleslaw, then fussed over the grill, which was one of the old-fashioned ones with charcoal. It was already burning red-hot, perfect for cooking the burgers that waited in the refrigerator below deck. It was crazy to be this worked up over the food, when it was likely to be the last thing on anyone's mind. But it was easier to think about potato salad than the past.

There was nothing else to do but wait. He paced the deck, and when that seemed too confined, moved to the dock and paced up and down that. He finally spotted the rental car as it pulled into the parking lot and his older brothers emerged. They were halfway down the dock when Daniel's familiar SUV turned into the lot. Patrick wasn't the least bit surprised that his twin was still driving the same car he'd had for years. Daniel had always claimed a car was nothing more than transportation. He'd never cared about style or speed.

"Here's Daniel now," Patrick said quietly to Ryan, Sean and Michael.

They all turned to watch their brother as he walked to the dock, then caught sight of them and hesitated, a dawning sense of recognition on his face.

"Too late to turn back now," Patrick said, going to meet his twin just in case Daniel had any crazy ideas about fleeing.

Daniel searched his brother's face, then drew him into a fierce hug. When the embrace ended, he met Patrick's gaze. "Tell me I'm not dreaming. Are those . . . ?" His voice caught.

"They're our brothers," Patrick told him.

"When? How? Why the hell didn't you say something?"

Patrick grinned at the litany of questions. "I'll let them explain, unless you're planning to stand here at the end of the dock all afternoon trying to figure it out on your own."

A grin spread across his twin's face. "You sound like your old self."

Patrick thought about that, then released a sigh. "You know, I'm beginning to feel like my old self, only better."

"Complete?" Daniel asked.

Patrick nodded. "That's it."

"I know. That's the way I felt the second I heard your voice on the phone. Next time you get some fool idea in your head about losing touch, I'm not going to let you get away with it."

Patrick leveled a gaze at him and thought of Alice. "There won't be a next time," he assured Daniel.

"Hey, you two going to stand down there all day?" Ryan called out. "Sean here is starved."

"Sean's always starved," Michael noted, poking his brother in the ribs.

Patrick led Daniel to the boat, made the introductions, then stood back while his older brothers peppered Daniel with questions until his head was no doubt spinning. Being here with all of them felt right, as if this day had been way too long coming. The only thing that could possibly have improved on it would have been having Alice here by his side.

Just as that wish crossed his mind, he thought he heard a whisper of sound on shore. He turned, but caught only a fleeting glimpse of movement. He couldn't prove it, of course, but it had been Alice. He knew it. He should have known he'd piqued her curiosity. He knew he'd stirred Molly's when he'd bought the food for today. Obviously, they'd put two and two together, and Alice, at least, hadn't been able to resist coming by to confirm their suspicions. He suspected Molly was a hundred miles away. That was the distance she preferred to keep between herself and Daniel.

Suddenly Ryan was by his side. "Brooding over Alice?" he asked.

Patrick shook his head. "I'm going to make things right with her."

"When?"

"Tomorrow."

"Good for you. Maggie's anxious to come up to meet her. I convinced her to stay home today, but by next week there'll be no holding her back."

"Tell her if she waits a few weeks, she could come for a wedding," Patrick said. "I don't intend to let Alice drag her heels."

Ryan grinned. "Think she might try?"

"She will if she's smart," Patrick said. "But I can be pretty persuasive when I set my mind to it."

Ryan's expression sobered. "That might be a good time to get together with the folks. Weddings always bring out the best in families."

Patrick promptly shook his head. "I'm not taking any chances with mine."

"You sure you want to get married without at least inviting them?"

"I'm sure," he said with conviction. "That doesn't mean you all can't get together with them while you're here. I'm sure Daniel will set it up." In fact, if he knew anything at all about his twin, Daniel would be eager to do it. It was probably taking every ounce of restraint he possessed not to call them right now.

"We'll play it by ear," Ryan said. "We've waited this long for an explanation of why they abandoned us. A few weeks or even months longer won't make any difference. It's a big decision, and we all need to be agreed that the timing's right."

Patrick gave his brother a grateful smile. "Thanks for understanding."

"Trust me, we all understand what a mixed bag of emotions are getting stirred up here. And none of us are all that anxious to hear why we were left behind. It's enough for now that we've seen Daniel again."

Patrick's gaze drifted to where his twin was laughing with Sean and Michael and felt his heart fill to bursting. "Yeah," he told Ryan. "That's enough for now."

Alice was staring out her classroom window at the turbulent June sky. It was going to storm any minute now. She ought to pack up her papers and head for home before the clouds opened up, but the prospect of going back to that empty house held no appeal. At least here at school there were other teachers in the building.

She'd been expecting Patrick to turn up ever since the end of the graduation ceremony, but there'd been no sign of him. Apparently, it was a promise he didn't intend to keep. She shouldn't be disappointed, but she was, especially after the scene she'd witnessed on his boat the day before. It had reduced her to tears and stirred hope in her heart once more.

A tap on the door startled her. When she turned, she was even more stunned to see Patrick in the doorway.

"You busy?" he asked.

Unable to find her tongue, she simply shook her head. He looked fabulous. Overnight it seemed as if his tan had deepened, so that his eyes seemed even bluer. He looked more carefree, too, as if a weight had been lifted from his shoulders. It took every ounce of restraint she possessed not to race across the room and throw herself into his arms.

He came in, glanced around at the small chairs meant for five-year-olds and settled for perching on the corner of her desk. That put him close enough that she could feel the heat radiating from him and smell his familiar masculine scent. She wanted desperately to reach out and rest her hand on the hard muscle of his thigh. Instead she sat perfectly still and waited impatiently to hear what was on his mind.

"You look beautiful," he said quietly.

"Thank you."

"I meant to be here right after graduation, but Ricky caught up with me and asked if I'd come to his party over at Jess's. I broke away as soon as I could."

"I see."

He held her gaze. "I've missed you."

"I saw you on Friday," she reminded him.

"But it's been longer than that since we were together, since we were on the same wavelength."

"True."

"I've been using the time to do some thinking."

"That's always good," she said, since he seemed to be waiting for a response.

"I saw my brothers yesterday. Daniel was there, too."

Alice blinked back tears. "I know. I saw."

He grinned. "I thought I saw you. I should have guessed you'd figure out something was up and poke around until you found out what it was."

She shrugged. "I care. Sue me." She studied him intently. "How did it go?"

"Awkwardly at first, but then it was like it was when they came here to meet me, almost as if we'd never been apart. I guess the bond between brothers is more powerful than I ever realized."

"And the bond between parent and child?"

"I'm still thinking about that one."

"With an open mind?"

He grinned. "At least as open a mind as any hardheaded man can have."

"Was there some other reason you wanted to see me today?" she asked.

He swallowed, then glanced toward the blackboard. "Do teachers still make kids write on the blackboard when they've misbehaved?"

"Sometimes," she said. "It's a little hard with kindergarten kids. They can't print or spell that well."

He grinned and stood up. "I can't say much for my handwriting, but my spelling's pretty good." He walked over, picked up a piece of chalk and began to write.

Alice held her breath as the words began to form.

Patrick Devaney loves Alice Newberry.

He turned to face her, a hopeful expression in his eyes. "How many times do you want me to write it?"

Her own eyes swimming with tears, she stood up. "Just say it."

Eyes locked with hers, he took a step toward her. "I love you, Alice Newberry," he said softly.

Alice tilted her head at the sound of the sweet words she'd wondered if she would ever hear. "Say it again."

"I love you," he repeated dutifully. "How many more times?"

"A million will do," she said.

"That could take forever," he pointed out.

She grinned at him. "I have the time. How about you?"

"Only if you'll marry me. And in case the fact that I love you is not enough incentive, I have it on good authority that I can get my brothers to come to the wedding."

"All of them?" she asked cautiously.

He nodded. "All of them."

"And your parents?"

"I'm not sure I'm ready to invite them to the wedding, but I promise that I'm working on forgiving them," he said, his expression neutral. "There's a lot of water under the bridge. Is the promise that I'll try good enough for now?"

Alice threw her arms around him. "Trying is the most I'll ever ask of you." She met his gaze. "That and that you'll never stop loving me."

He brushed a stray curl away from her cheek, then gave her one of those devastating Devaney smiles. "Darlin', that one's easy."

Epilogue

Alice had drawn on every bit of persuasive skill she possessed to try to convince Molly to be the maid of honor at her wedding. She'd even gotten Patrick into the act, hoping he could charm Molly into reconsidering the firm "No" she'd uttered each time Alice had asked.

"I wish you all the luck and happiness in the world. You know I do," Molly told Alice when she made one last plea. "But I can't do it, not if Daniel's going to be there, and especially not if he's going to be Patrick's best man."

"But how can I possibly get married without you as my maid of honor?" Alice asked. She could see the stubborn light shining in Molly's eyes and knew she was defeated.

"You pick someone else and walk down that aisle with your head held high and your eyes focused on your handsome groom, that's how," Molly said. "I'll be thinking of you every second."

"You won't even come to the wedding?" Alice asked.

"I can't," Molly said. "I wish I could, but it's not possible. If that's being selfish, I'm sorry."

"You're not being selfish," Alice insisted, giving her a fierce hug. "And I'm the one who should be sorry. I shouldn't have tried to put you in that position, knowing it would make you miserable."

Molly gave her a halfhearted smile. "It was nice to be asked," she said, then added wistfully, "I love weddings."

"You'll have your own, one of these days, and you'll be the most beautiful bride Widow's Cove has ever seen," Alice assured her.

"A pretty thought, but you don't have to butter me up. I'll still do all the cooking for the rehearsal dinner."

Alice regarded her with surprise. "You agreed to have it here?"

"As if Patrick would give me a choice in the matter," Molly said. "But I've brought in help for the night. I'll be far away."

"Licking your wounds," Alice said.

"So what if I am? Believe me, I'm entitled."

"I just wish the wounds had healed by now. If they run that deep, they could infect the rest of your life. If you'd only talk about what happened between you and Daniel, maybe you could move on."

Molly frowned at her. "I have moved on. I just don't care to set eyes on that weasel ever again."

Alice grinned at the heat in her voice. "Yes, you've moved on all right. I can hear it in your tone."

"I have," Molly insisted.

"Then you could catch a glimpse of Daniel and not have it turn you inside out?"

"Of course."

Alice regarded her with a speculative look. "I'll keep that in mind."

"Don't go getting any wild ideas," Molly said, alarm in her eyes. "Concentrate on your wedding and leave my life to me."

"Oh, I have plenty of time for both," Alice assured her.

"Not if you expect to live to see your wedding day," Molly said, her expression grim.

It was the heartfelt sincerity behind her words that told Alice everything she needed to know. Molly wasn't over Daniel. Not by a long shot. Maybe their relationship couldn't be fixed, but Alice had never let long odds stop her from trying. Besides, she was deep in the throes of her own bridal joy. She couldn't be totally content until everyone around her was just as happy. Unfortunately, in this instance, she might have to wait till after her own wedding to pull it off.

Patrick's nerves had been pretty much shot by the time Alice finally walked down the aisle and stood next to him. He hadn't believed they were going to pull it off until he actually heard her say, "I do," and the priest pronounced them man and wife. Then he let out a whoop of joy that could be heard in the next county.

Alice grinned at him. "I hope I always make you this happy," she said, her tone dry.

"No question about that," he said as he took her

hand and marched her out of the church. Outside on the steps, he pulled her into his arms and gave her the kind of kiss he'd feared would send the priest into heart failure.

When he finally released her, he tucked a finger under her chin and looked into her eyes. "I love you, Alice Devaney."

She rested her hand against his cheek. Her fingers were trembling. "I love you, Patrick Devaney. And all your brothers."

He gave her a searching look. "Even Daniel?"

"Why wouldn't I love Daniel?"

"Because he hurt Molly. Even I have a hard time with that one."

"We're going to fix it," she said with confidence.

"Maybe we should concentrate on us," he said, regarding her worriedly. "Molly and Daniel are adults. They can fix their own problems, assuming they even want to."

"But I want everyone to be as happy as we are."

"Not possible," he told her, pulling her close for another kiss. "No one on earth could ever be as happy as we are."

"Speak for yourself," Ryan said, coming up to slap him on the back and give Alice a kiss. "Maggie and I are doing okay."

"So are Deanna and I," Sean said, joining them.

"And Kelly and I aren't doing so bad in the joy department, either," Michael chimed in.

They all turned to look at Daniel, who simply stared. "What?"

"There's something missing from your life, little brother," Ryan said.

Patrick gave him a sympathetic look. "You might as well go with the flow, Daniel. Besides, they'll be back in Boston soon. That's too far away for any meddling."

"But I'm here," Alice said, regarding her new brother-in-law speculatively.

Daniel frowned at her. "Meddle at your own peril. I'm a hard case."

"So was I," Patrick pointed out, tightening his arm around Alice's waist. "Look at me now."

"See," Alice said. "Look at all these fine examples your brothers have set for you."

Patrick saw the fire in Daniel's eyes and knew Alice was about to push him too far. He wanted nothing to spoil this day, so he cut off her words with another kiss.

"I think we should be getting to the reception," he said. "I want to dance with my bride."

Alice looked up at him, a question in her eyes, but then she sighed with understanding. "I guess I only get to fix one thing in this family at a time."

He grinned at her. "You've done more than your share with me. Let Daniel take care of himself."

"I suppose," she agreed with obvious reluctance.

"I'll make it worth your while," he teased.

Immediately her eyes lit up. "How?"

281

"I'll show you tonight."

"Why not now? I'm told there's a room at the Widow's Cove Hotel with our name on it."

"And a room downstairs filled with guests waiting to toast to our happiness," he said, fighting temptation.

"Just think how much happier we'll be if we take a little detour," she said.

"You have a very wicked mind," he told her.

"Does that bother you?"

"Not as long as I'm the only one in those wild fantasies of yours."

"The only one," she assured him. "Always and forever."

Forever, Patrick thought, and waited for the first twinge of panic. It never came. Instead, all he felt was contentment and anticipation. Their life was going to be one hell of a ride.

SHERRYL WOODS has written more than seventy-five novels. She also operates her own bookstore, Potomac Sunrise, in Colonial Beach, Virginia. If you can't visit Sherryl at her store, then be sure to drop her a note at P.O. Box 490326, Key Biscayne, FL 33149 or check out her Web site at www.sherrylwoods.com.

Center Point Publishing
600 Brooks Road ● PO Box 1
Thorndike ME 04986-0001 USA

(207) 568-3717

US & Canada:
1 800 929-9108
www.centerpointlargeprint.com